BLOOD IN THE WATER

MARK MASZTAL

MARK MASZTAL

Published by
Not Dog Books
Office of Publication:
256 Gillette Avenue, Springfield, MA 01118 USA
notdogcomics.com

First Edition: November 2020
ISBN 978-1-7330144-1-0

BLOOD IN THE WATER

This book is dedicated to my father-in-law, Edward Korovae (RIP).
He loved to read, and I think he would have liked this book.

I'd like to thank Michael Dobbs, Karen St. Onge,
Steve Murphy and Mike Murray for their editorial guidance
and friendship.

Thanks to John Amenta and Jon Johnson for
being my shark brothers.

To Speilberg, Benchley, Gottlieb, de Guzman, and Dreyfuss
for stirring my imagination.

And to my wife Kathy. She is my rock and she showed me
it's okay to use commas.

I wasn't planning on writing a book but it came out of the depths,
and dared me to write it.

MARK MASZTAL

BLOOD IN THE WATER

Books are sharks . . . because sharks have been around for a very long time. There were sharks before there were dinosaurs, and the reason sharks are still in the ocean is that nothing is better at being a shark than a shark.

Douglas Adams

MARK MASZTAL

Chapter 1

Matt Cooper was tired.

He was goddamn tired and still could not figure out why he was on the *Polaris II* on another 6-month excursion. He was the CEO and Chairman for the Cooper Institute for Shark Research. He was bored with life and thought a new tour on the *Polaris II* would energize his life. Was he wrong? The original *Polaris* was a wonderful scientific vessel and when you worked it for six months, you worked. The new *Polaris II* was a hotel on the water. State of the art scientific computers and labs and all the bells and whistles any marine biologist would want or desire to make their work easier. But the *Polaris II* was also outfitted with a small pool and at least two Jacuzzi's as well as a 4-star chef and banquet facility. Hell, there were at least three popcorn machines somewhere below decks and one topside. Damn millennials felt like they deserved anything they could get and they never stopped asking for more. This was a goddamn research vessel, not a Caribbean cruise.

Cooper rolled out of his bunk... actually it was a queen size posture-correcting mattress with box spring. Being the CEO had its perks. He also had the largest stateroom on the ship, located at the stern, so saying it was his bunk was being sarcastic. The digital alarm clock on the nightstand read 6:07 am. Why was he up so early? He actually never slept well when he was on the water. It didn't matter if it was a large vessel or a small runabout. He'd spent most of his adult life either on or under the water, and sleeping was never something he ever fully achieved.

He put on his glasses and pulled a simple cotton robe over his t-shirt and lounge pants. He looked over to the full-length mirror on the wall and took a good look at his 71-year-old self. *"My God, when did I get old?"*. The man staring back at him was 30 pounds overweight, his beard was white and his ginger, curly hair had receded to the top of his head and had also turned white.

At least he had his health. Remarkably, his blood pressure was good, his cholesterol was under control, and he quit drinking years ago so his liver function was top notch. For the amount of diving he'd done over the years, his lungs were strong, and the daily swims he took kept him in decent shape.

He looked back over to his bed and gave up on going back to sleep. He might as well head down to the labs to see what biological miracles had occurred while he slept.

He left his stateroom and walked into a wall. Actually a human wall. Specialist Mark Markowski was one of the newest recruits on the *Polaris II*. His specialty was document management and Information Technology. He worked miracles on the computer system and satellite network. He stood 6' 5" and topped the scales at 275lbs. He was in his mid 50's with glasses, short brown greying hair and a white billy-goat beard. He was in good shape for a big man who spent most of his time sitting behind a desk or snaking cables under and behind workstations. Cooper had seen him speed walking the decks in the early morning, and saw that he was not a fan of the on-board gym. The gym rats turned him off.

"Good morning, Doctor Cooper."

"Good morning, Mark, and please, you can call me Matt."

"Oh, sure...but I can't do that. I have too much respect for you and the work that you've done over the years."

"Well, I respect you, Mark," Cooper said, "And the work that you've done on the *Polaris II*. But I want to keep our relationship friendly, so I will call you Mark, is that alright?"

"Of course it is..."

"But?" Cooper asked.

"Would you mind calling me Paper?"

"Paper?"

"Yes, sir. It's a screen name that I'm known by on message boards and forums."

"Alright..." Cooper laughed. There was the laugh he remembered.

He had not heard it in a long time. It was his friendly chuckle; at least it wasn't his big donkey laugh.

"...Paper, it is."

"Great, thank you, sir."

"So what's going on today, Paper?"

Paper looked down to the digital tablet that he was carrying. "It's actually a light day today for myself and the lab. All the servers are running well, no glitches lately, the satellite network is on point, and data transfer has gone uninterrupted.

"Higgins and Kohi are prepping the shark cradle for some afternoon tagging: Doctors Martin and Cassidy had been running some blood cultures all night that were crunching some serious terabytes."

"Well," Cooper said, "that sounds like an unexciting overnight and a possible fun afternoon." He looked up at Paper with a questioning look. "You said Higgins and Kohi?"

"Yes, Doctor Cooper."

"Ahem."

"Yes, Matt."

"Anything else Paper - and why on Earth are you up so early?"

"It's a sleeping thing," Paper said. "I always have problems sleeping in a new bed. At least I brought my own water pillow. That's the only thing that helps me get any sleep at all. I was up early and couldn't get comfortable, so I figured it was easier to get up than trying to get back to sleep."

"Then that makes us two peas in a pod. I couldn't sleep either, so I'm going up to the bridge to check in with Captain Dobbs, and then take a shower and have some breakfast."

"Alright, Matt. I'm heading down to the computer lab to check on the servers and I'll see you at breakfast."

Cooper watched Paper Markowski walk down the hall and enter one of the staircases heading to the tech labs.

Higgins and Kohi. Two very good marine biologists he was lucky to have onboard the *Polaris II*. He stole them from the Florida Institute of Technology. They had some breakthrough results in shark migration and behaviors and he offered them six months of diehard science without the politics and academia of a large campus like FIT. He also offered to fund their work for the next two years if they signed on.

Higgins jumped at it, but Kohi took a little more time. She said she needed to make sure that she would have a career to go back to. But deep down Cooper felt that Kohi's Japanese upbringing and being the only daughter to very controlling parents weighed on what Himari Kohi decided. She wanted to be the good daughter and do what they wanted, but deep down she was a damn good marine biologist. She was quite brilliant, and Cooper was glad she followed her career and dream and came onboard. He also felt the relationship between Kohi and Doctor Charlie Higgins was more than just colleagues. There were no rumors, but he didn't get to be 71 years old and the CEO of The Cooper Institute for Shark Research and not see signs, slight as they were. It was fine with him because he also really liked Charlie Higgins. He was tall, good looking, and treated everyone with respect, especially Himari. They worked well together and were professional so he never thought there would be any romantic distractions in their work. Work had its place and their personal life was for after hours.

Chapter 2

The bridge of the *Polaris II* was large. 30 feet across and 25 feet deep. The front and sides of the room were all windows giving anyone on duty a fantastic view. The back wall contained radio equipment and storage as well as a restroom and a stairway down to the lower decks. Cooper came in from one of the two side doors. Both led to decks that ran along the sides of the bridge stack. It was early so there weren't many crewmembers on duty.

Captain Robert Dobbs was at his usual chair set higher than all the others because the man demanded a clear view. The boat was his baby and he wanted to see everything. Dobbs was older than most of the crew, hitting the 65-year mark a few months prior, but he was in good shape, probably a bit heavier than he wanted to be. He had the old-man-in-the-sea grey beard and short, greying hair. He liked his cardigan sweaters and cargo pants and like always, he had his Captain's hat on.

Seated behind him was navigator Kyle Richards who helped keep the ship going in the right direction. Beside him was pilot Marty Malone. Both men were in there 30's and had previous naval experience. Radioman John Amenta was seated in back next to the radio unit and was intently listening to a broadcast; his eyes were focused on what only he could hear.

"Good morning, Captain Dobbs" said Cooper.

Dobbs swung around in his modified barber's Captain's chair.

"How are ya Mister Cooper, up a bit early aren't ya?"

"I guess so, Captain, couldn't sleep. Where are we?"

"We're approximately 76 miles off the coast of Queensland, Australia, Mister Cooper, heading into the Coral Sea. We had an uneventful overnight, and all seems quiet this morning. I hear the chef is going to have some amazing..."

"Captain Dobbs!" shouted Amenta.

"What is it Mister, can't you see I'm talking?" Dobbs barked.

"Sorry, Captain, I'm getting a distress call from the Gloria J, a fishing vessel 12 miles northwest of us. She's reporting deaths and vessel damage. They say they're sinking and they don't dare launch their lifeboat or hit the water in survival suits."

"What?!" Captain Dobbs yelled.

Deaths? Sinking? No lifeboat or suits?

"What's going on, Mister?!"

"Their radioman says...."

"What is it man?"

"It's sharks, sir... lots of sharks."

"Get on the horn, let them know we're on our way, then announce rescue stations, all hands on deck. I want rescue teams ready to get wet and I want medical personnel ready to receive patients.... understand, Amenta?"

"Yes sir, on the double!"

"Haul your ass or you'll be wearing my size 10!"

"Amenta" asked Cooper, "what did they say about sharks?"

The radioman turned around to address Cooper. Amenta was in his mid 30's with a heavy build, glasses and a jet-black beard.

"Just that there were a lot of them. All different kinds; whites, makos, tigers, hammers...."

"What kind of ship did you say it was?"

"A commercial fishing vessel with long nets."

Cooper looked towards Dobbs. "That would make sense. The sharks would be drawn to the fish struggling in the nets. If any fish were bleeding, the sharks would follow the scent right to the ship. But deaths, and a sinking vessel?"

Amenta said, "Their radioman said there was a big one."

"A big one?" Both Dobbs and Cooper exclaimed.

The crew of the *Polaris II* did hop to it and within 15 minutes the ship's rail was full of binocular spotters, as well as a sonar man and a radar operator on the bridge. The rescue team had reported that they were ready on the stern's lower deck and Doctor Helen Shane, chief medical officer, reported that they were well supplied and ready for any and all traumas.

Chapter 3

At twelve knots the *Polaris II* took an hour to get to the fishing vessel. What the crew of the ship could not expect was the carnage and devastation they would find. The Gloria J was a 100-foot long net commercial vessel and currently most of her was underwater. Part of the bow was above water and that was where the survivors were huddled. A few were wearing survival suits, but most of the seven crewmen were wearing hooded rain slickers, hats, and gloves. A few were holding injured limbs or compression bandages while two crew-members were lying on their backs with bandages on a leg and torso, respectively.

The crew of the *Polaris II* was crowding onto the observation rails, shocked by what they saw, and completely devastated by what was in the water: an oil slick all around the boat as well as torn netting and scattered fish. But the deepest shock came from the blood mingling with the water, some of it pooling and some of it dispersing in the waves. The most disturbing however, were the body parts. Hunks of flesh were floating, pink and mottled, while the occasional limb was seen in the wreckage along with a few gnawed torsos. Retching sounds came from the crew of the *Polaris II* and quite a few crewmembers ran inside to hide from the horror in the water.

Cooper was standing on the rail next to Captain Dobbs and Executive Officer Steven Menard while a spotter named Coache was describing to them the details he saw through his binoculars.

"I spot two crew members down, possibly unconscious while the other five seem all right but some are injured. I don't see any sharks, but there is a lot of blood and body parts in the water to attract them. If we're going to make a rescue, we'll need at least two of the Zodiac Emergency Response Boats."

"What do you think, XO?" Dobbs asked.

"Captain, I'll put my best man on the sonar to assure us there are no sharks and zero risk to our rescue team, and then I'll get those poor souls onboard and have their wounds tended to."

Captain Dobbs turned to Matt, "Now that, Mister Cooper, is why you let me pick my crew."

"No question there, Captain".

Steven Menard was ex-Navy. He had spent 15 years in the service and enjoyed it, but he had suffered a few knee injuries and decided it was time to retire. He was average height with short sandy haircut high and tight with a blond Tom Selleck mustache. His frame was sturdy and fit but walked with a slight limp.

He had played his golf and fished until they no longer held any interest and contemplated opening a beachside bar when Dobbs came calling nine months after retirement and offered him the XO position on a science vessel. The paycheck Dobbs promised him was double what he made in the Navy and it was a more relaxed environment onboard the *Polaris II*. It took him less than ten seconds to say yes. He found Captain Dobbs to be a kind man, but also one that knew his business and could kick ass when needed. They made a good team.

Cooper stared out at the horror and destruction before him. How could this happen and what did the radioman from The Gloria J mean by 'a big one'? He's going to have to talk to that crew, none of this made any sense to him. Different species of sharks don't swim together unless they're in the middle of a feeding frenzy. Single species will swim together usually during mating. Black nose sharks will maintain relationships, but they are selective. Sand tiger sharks will gather in groups of five or six, but only to mate. Whites and hammerheads are generally solitary creatures, not even swimming with their same species. There have never been reports of different species of sharks swimming together and never attacking as an organized group. There is something historical going on here and Matthew Cooper, head honcho of the Cooper Institute for Shark Research, was going to find out what.

The rescue of the Gloria J. survivors didn't take long. The sonar came back clear of any large signals giving the rescue teams time to get the injured loaded into the ERB's that had been launched by the ships rear crane. They made it back to the ship and down to the sickbay where Doctor Shane and her staff tended to their wounds.

Cooper was truly concerned about the welfare of the surviving crew, but what he really wanted to ask them about, what he needed to ask them about, was any information about the sharks that attacked them. Unfortunately the radioman had not survived, so it was going to be a matter of interviewing all the surviving crewmembers and compiling their statements into some kind of general report. Cooper was an easy man to talk to, but he had to wait like everyone else. Doctor Shane was a fair woman; she was quite liked by the crew of the *Polaris II*, but was not to be crossed when it came to her patient's care.

Cooper joined Captain Dobbs and Menard while they stood looking through the windows of the sickbay. They too were chomping at the bit to speak with the crew. The captain and the chief engineer of the Gloria J had not survived: that left the deck boss, and a few deckhands and greenhorns to be interviewed.

Doctor Helen Shane was in her mid-fifties, slight with dark black collar length hair that had started to see some streaking of grey. She had a serious face, but it was said that when she smiled, everyone smiled with her. She was not smiling and her face seemed even more serious than usual.

She came out of the infirmary and approached the three men.

"Captain, gentlemen, what we've got here are some badly injured patients and I feel the two most gravely injured won't survive the trip back to Australia unless I operate".

Captain Dobbs said, "Doctor, can you tell us what happened? Have any of the men said anything?"

"What about the sharks?" Cooper asked.

Doctor Shane looked at Cooper, "Is that all you can think of right now Mister Cooper? Don't you have any decency? These men are injured, dying, and all you can ask me is about is sharks?"

"Doctor, that's not what I meant and I apologize for my comment. What I meant to say is how are the men and can any of them talk about what happened? We need to find out any details that they can give us."

"I think what Mister Cooper is saying Doctor Shane, is that we're all very concerned about the welfare of your patients," said Captain Dobbs. "We all want to make sure that no one else dies and that your patients recover from their wounds. However, I have the safety of the crew of the *Polaris II* to think about and we will need to talk to any man in your care that can give us any pertinent information."

"We know there was a large school of sharks and that they attacked the Gloria J. We have also heard from their radioman about a very large shark. We need to get as much info as we can. Please let us know when we can speak with your patients."

"Captain Dobbs, I'll ask the few conscious patients what they know, but for right now they are either in physical or mental shock. It's going to be at least a day–"

"A day?" blurted out Cooper.

"Yes Mister Cooper, a day. I know this is your ship, but I've been onboard for a lot longer than you've graced us with your presence, so let me do my job and see to my patients. I'll let you know when any of them can speak. For now I have to scrub-in for surgery. I think one man is going to lose his leg and the other one has internal bleeding, so I'm going to be up to my elbows in blood and I do not want see any of your faces until I say so, am I clear?"

"Crystal, Doctor," Cooper, replied.

"Yes, thank you Doctor. I'll make sure no one interrupts you or bothers your patients. Good luck with your surgeries," Captain Dobbs said.

With that, Doctor Shane spun on her heel and went back into her infirmary.

Captain Dobbs turned to Cooper, "Matt, I know what you want, but you've got to let her have her way. I want answers too, but we need her clearance to speak with the crewmembers, okay?"

"Yeah, I got you Cap, I got a bit over excited. I was a bit of an asshole," Cooper said.

"Yes you were," Menard said.

Both Dobbs and Cooper turned to look at the XO, who until now had been silent.

"He speaks –" Cooper said.

"There you go again - asshole," Menard said and he turned and left the hallway for the staircase to the bridge.

"I'm just making tons of friends today aren't I?" Cooper stated.

Captain Dobbs gave him a silent stink-eye and followed the XO up to the bridge leaving Cooper alone in the hallway.

The operating room on the *Polaris II* is state-of-the-art containing everything from a CT scanner to a high tech diagnostic system for tracing and breaking apart DNA strands. The only thing missing was an open MRI, and Doctor Shane knew some of the medical staff were still hoping for one.

Shane's first patient was deckhand Eddie Ortiz, diagnosed with internal bleeding. A chest tube had been inserted to relieve the pressure and allow the patient to stabilize enough for exploratory surgery. The CAT scan showed bleeding near his spleen and that was where she started. Ortiz's spleen had been ruptured and the easiest path to his recovery was removal of the organ. He'll have to be cautious about getting infections and eat several small meals during the day, but Doctor Shane expected a full recovery.

The other serious patient was greenhorn Henry Wilson. He was a good-looking kid of nineteen and was in serious trouble. A shark, or many sharks had mauled his left leg below the knee. Doctor Shane had made sure that he had been stabilized and was preparing for a lower leg amputation. She and her staff had seen their fair share of shark bites; there were many a crewmember on the *Polaris II* that had scars from both bites and stitches.

Wilson's lower left leg looked like hamburger. The tibia had been cracked apart in three places, with bone fragments around the wound. The fibula, the smaller outer bone of the leg, was gone, ripped out from its base at the ankle and the lower knee. There was massive tissue loss. Nerves, arteries and capillaries had been shredded. Doctor Shane decided there was not enough leg to save. Wilson was a young, strong man, so recovery should be uneventful.

The surgery went well; blood loss was kept to a minimum and the amputation was clean. Doctor Shane had enough skin tissue left to make a perfect cap over the stump. So far modern medicine had succeeded in fending off Mister Death.

Chapter 4

Twenty-four hours went by very slowly on the *Polaris II* while crew members went about their daily routines, marine biologists and their assistants continued with their experiments, and Matt Cooper sat on deck looking at the remains of the Gloria J. XO Menard had his men retrieving debris from the wreck, hoping to find some clues to what happened while they waited for Doctor Shane to provide them some answers.

The rest of the Gloria J had dipped below the waves leaving an oil slick, tangled fishing nets and debris on the water's surface. Any body parts that had not been scavenged by the local sea life had been retrieved and placed in plastic bags for later analysis. Larger pieces of debris had been removed so as not to cause any hazards for other local vessels. In another day there would be no signs that anything terrible had happened.

Cooper leaned on the railing of the watch deck looking out at a sea that he had spent the last sixty years either above or below. He started the institute because of his love of sharks. He had always been fascinated with them since he was a young teen. He put his heart, his soul and a lot of his, and his family's money, into starting the Institute so research could be done to learn as much as they could about sharks, rays and their families.

Matt Cooper had grown up wealthy. His family had been investors, lawyers and financial planners for decades. Their gross family worth was larger than most small countries. Matt never had to want for anything, and yet it never made him happy. He had always been infatuated with the sea. Anytime the family spent time at one of its seaside homes, he would spend all of his time outside in or near the water.

He read as many books as he could about fish, whales, crustaceans and, especially, sharks. He didn't know why but maybe it was because they were dangerous - something which excited him but confused his family.

His father, Jerome, was a very serious man. He always wanted what was best for his family, which was why he was never home. Either he was at the office, away on investment trips or socializing with other wealthy people. Making connections and doing deals was in his blood. His lovely wife, Madison, was also no slouch when it came to making partnerships to increase the family's earnings. Her family was in politics, so she had other affiliations, besides bankers. Her family dealt in partisan and bi-partisan deals, always looking to improve their standing, and to always be on top. Her father was a United States Senator and as such, he sat on many committees and had associates in the Pentagon. Military contracts flowed into her husband's businesses, and the Cooper family took advantage of all of them.

Matt grew up with two brothers, Alan, four years his senior, and Richard, three years younger.

Alan was the serious one, the good looking one that had his parents wrapped around his finger because he knew where the money came from, and he wanted to be a large part of it.

Richard, or Richie as he liked to be called, was a free spirit, directionless, but he knew that he loved Matt and hated Alan. Alan who had always looked down on him and bullied him. Matt always stood up for Richie as he would take no shit from Alan. Matt was a little shorter than Alan, but he was stockier and stronger and had a wicked temper. Alan had been on the receiving end of a few short fights with Matt, and Matt always ended up with a belt across his back from his father.

Jerome did not understand his middle son's love of the ocean and marine life. He had no scientific interests, because in his mind it would never make any money.

As the boys got older Alan went to work in the family business.

Matt went to the best schools for Marine Biology. His grades were excellent, top of all of his classes; he had won lots of grants and his school choices gave him a free ride. He wanted to prove to his family that he could make something of himself that did not include the family money.

Richie was Matt's tagalong, not excelling like his brother, but just getting by with his grades and athletics. Richie had grown up to be a good-looking young man with an athlete's physique and a kind heart. Matt was always proud of his little brother, they were best of friends.

While vacationing off the coast of Cape Cod, on Pearl Island, Matt and Richie were invited to join a small group of shark researchers. The boys' parents were not exactly thrilled about Richie going out to sea with his older brother, but by the time they found out, the boys were already at sea. It was to be a one-month study off the coast of Nova Scotia on a mid-sized boat called *The Neville*. Besides Matt and Richie, there were seven others onboard.

Matt had been instructing Richie on how to scuba dive and to use his athlete's lungs to free swim. Matt had always been a good swimmer and Richie was doing his best to keep up with, not to compete with his older brother.

They had seen sharks as they dived but none of them paid any interest to the two divers. Matt and Richie had decided to go deeper than the other crew members had suggested. Neither man thought that going to 50-feet would hurt anything, so one morning they made ready and dived.

The water was murkier and colder than they would have liked, but they still saw some amazing sights. They were a bit surprised to see some tropical fish this far north. In the first half hour, they had spotted Yellow Butterfly fish, a couple of Shortfin Bigeye and some Flying Gurands burrowing into the silt on the ocean floor.

Matt was sifting through the ocean floor with a small net when a fish caught his eye, a fish that had no right to be there. He scooped the fish with a quick movement and when the silt settled he had a three-foot Longnose Chimaera in his net. The Chimaera were a deep-water species, rarely seen this far north. It was dark brown with a long stout body, a very long beak-like nose and the creepiest green eyes he had ever seen.

Richie had swum over to him to see the fish, when suddenly, he looked over Matt's shoulder in horror. A shark hit Matt square in the back, biting into his scuba gear and driving him forward. The shark's teeth became entangled in Matt's rig and began to shake him violently from side to side, trying to free it self.

Matt held onto his gears harness with one hand and pulled out his diver's knife from its scabbard with the other. He blindly stabbed behind him, sometimes missing the shark, sometimes stabbing it. He reversed the blade in his hand and stabbed down and behind, catching the shark in the jaw.

The shark made one final hard struggle and freed itself from the scuba gear and Matt's stinging blade.

Matt had a moment to orient himself when he saw Richie swimming towards him. He tried to warn him off, but the shark, a ten-foot great white, swam at his brother. The shark, infuriated that it had missed out on one meal, now saw a new target and charged towards Richie. Matt desperately tried to get to his brother, but the shark was too fast and took Richie in his side and bit down, releasing a huge cloud of bright red blood into the water. The shark shook its head a few times, Richie's arms and legs flailing in the water. The shark then swam away, with Richie Cooper in its mouth.

The funeral was a somber event, especially with the lack of a body. The rift between Matt, his father and brother widened. He was blamed for Richie's death, even though investigators deemed it an accident. Matt was the first son attacked, but it didn't matter to Jerome Cooper. His youngest son was dead, and Matt caused it. He believed if Richie had not been diving so deep, he would still be alive.

Matt's mother understood, and worried about Matt while grieving over the loss of her youngest boy. She quietly comforted Matt, knowing the repercussions she would have to bear if Jerome found out.

Matt returned to school and continued his studies, hoping they would keep his mind off of the death of his brother. His relationship with the two other men in the family never got better, but it stabilized for the good of the family. Family functions were tense, but everyone got along as best they could.

Matt spent more time away from home after college, shipping out on different research vessels, staying away for six months at a time. He kept to himself and put all of his time into studying the creature that destroyed his family. Money was still deposited into his bank account but he was committed to making a go of it on his own. He liked to tinker, and designed a different type of breather element for scuba gear that revolutionized the sport. He patented the design and leased the rights out to the many companies manufacturing the gear. The money started to roll in, setting him self up for a profitable future.

As the years went along, Cooper created more ground breaking inventions, as well as becoming a pioneer in shark research. When he thought the time was right, he bought some land in Florida and built the Cooper Institute for Shark Research. He had accomplished what he always wanted to do, to be his own man, with no one to answer to or pay back.

The only person he owed anything to was his brother Richie, whose portrait hung on the wall in the Institute's lobby.

Matt Cooper, scientist, adventurer, shark expert and now a frightened old man.

Doctor Helen Shane gave word to the bridge that she was ready to brief Captain Dobbs and Mister Cooper on her findings after the surgery of the two crewmen from the Gloria J. They all met in the conference room on C deck, directly above Cooper's stateroom at the stern of the ship. The large windows usually gave a spectacular view, but today all it gave was the memory of tragedy.

Doctor Shane had changed from her surgery scrubs into a pair of jeans, a black t-shirt and medical coat, her hair pulled back into a ponytail. The day's horror showed on her face.

"Gentlemen, let me start by saying we were lucky. Most of the survivors from the Gloria J have sustained only minor injuries and my staff saw to their needs. The two crewmen that required surgery came through fine and are in recovery. I had to perform a splenectomy on one and a below-the-knee amputation on the other. Both men are lucky to be alive."

Doctor Shane paused for a minute. She had rehearsed what she was about to say a few times, looking for some hope, but it wasn't to be found.

"Crewman Henry Wilson's lower leg was crushed, but not by the accident."

Captain Dobbs interjected. "Then what crushed it?"

"It was a shark attack, gentlemen. There were signs of tooth ser-rations along the remaining bone, and tissue loss was massive. There was no way to save his leg."

"Are you sure it was a shark attack Doctor," Cooper asked. "Until we speak to the crewmen we can't be sure,"

"I am 100 percent sure it was a shark attack and not by one shark, but many. I took bite mark measurements and spoke with some of the victims. It was multiple sharks that attacked them and not just one species. One crewmen confirmed there were tigers, hammerheads and great whites in the mix."

"I also found these." Doctor Shane reached into her lab coat and drew out a small-capped plastic vial and gave it a rattling shake.

"What's that?" asked Captain Dobbs.

"Shark teeth fragments, Captain," Shane said "I found them in Wilson's wounds. Some were mixed in with the flesh and muscle and a few tips were embedded in his remaining tibia. I originally thought the shards were Wilson's, but then I looked at them closer and discovered they were from the sharks."

Cooper asked, "And you're sure about this?"

"Absolutely positive that these shards are from a shark and not a human."

"Well that's freaking terrific!" Dobbs exclaimed. "Shit!" He walked away from the conference table to look out the stern windows.

"This just emphasizes how important it is that I speak to your patients. We have to know what happened out there and gather as many answers as possible."

"If it's samples you're looking for Mister Cooper, then I can help you with that," interjected XO Menard who was standing in the rooms open doorway.

Captain Dobbs turned towards his Executive Officer, "What have you got Steve?"

XO Menard entered the room and withdrew a clear plastic bag he was holding behind his back. He placed it on the conference table and stood at ease.

Everyone gathered around the bag on the table and studied it.

"*Holy shit*," Cooper said quietly.

Doctor Shane exhaled. Hours of stress flowed out of her body.

Captain Dobbs looked to Menard and then to Cooper.

"Coop, is that what I think it is?"

Cooper picked up the sealed bag and looked at a shark's tooth, one that was approximately four inches long with serrations on one side and a clean edge on the other. The tooth was pitted and had decay on it, signs of disease.

Captain Dobbs asked, "Where did you find this, Steve?"

"My men found it embedded in some of the timber we pulled out of the water. It was wedged in pretty tight, one of my guys had to use pliers to free it."

"What do you think, Matt?" Dobbs asked.

Captain Dobbs' formality had obviously been thrown out the window. He was dead serious about this find and wanted to let everyone know there was no screwing around this attack.

"Captain, what we've got here is a shark's tooth that I can't classify. It's bigger than any great white's tooth. Now before everyone starts talking Megalodon, their teeth were a bit larger, and of course they're extinct. I don't know where it came from, but I can tell you it's in rough shape."

Cooper continued, "There is some pitting on the tooth and serious discoloration. I'd say it's full of cavities and it has plaque all over it, but that doesn't happen with sharks. When their teeth get old and worn down, they drop out and another tooth replaces it up from the gum."

"I'd say this shark is sick, but without it I can't be more specific."

"All right," Captain Dobbs said, "Let's get you down to the labs with that tooth to run some tests. Doctor Shane, let me know when we can speak with your patients. This nightmare has just been dialed up to ten."

Captain Dobbs returned to the bridge of the *Polaris II*. The number of men and women on the bridge had doubled since the Gloria J incident and there was a steady buzz among the crewmembers.

XO Menard was standing at attention next to the Captain's chair and turned when he heard Dobbs approaching.

"Report."

"Captain, we are heading towards Brisbane to drop off the crew from the Gloria J. ETA is three hours."

"Excellent, Mister Menard." Dobbs said while in his chair. "How is our crew doing?"

"As well as can be expected, sir. Everyone is at his or her stations and the boat is running top notch. I haven't seen any real problems, but some of the salvage crew is a little spooked. They saw some nasty shit when they were dredging the wreckage from the Gloria J. I made sure those men had some downtime to get their heads straight."

"Very good, Mister Menard," Captain Dobbs said.

"Steven, step closer," said Dobbs in a low voice as he turned to his XO. "What do you think happened out there? I know you don't say much but your eyes see everything, that's why I hired you. You've seen enough crazy shit to have an opinion."

"Captain," Menard said, "I don't like to assume, but by my observations, the Gloria J was attacked by a large herd of sharks that wrecked the boat, killed most of the crew. That of course is stating the obvious, but I also feel we are sailing towards something no one has ever seen. Not our highly paid scientists, and not our Mister Cooper."

"Thank you for your viewpoint, Mister Menard," said Dobbs. "And as for our earlier conversation with Mister Cooper, I will not agree with you in front of the crew, but your observation at that moment was spot on."

XO Menard nodded his head and looked out at the Coral Sea as they headed towards Brisbane.

Chapter 5

Matt Cooper was in Marine Bio Lab Two sitting at a counter with a microscope, assorted probes, medical wipes, test tubes and sample containers. Also in front of him on a stainless steel sample tray was the large shark's tooth and the tooth fragments that Doctor Shane had removed from crewman Wilson's leg. The fragments had been laid out on a smaller paper-lined tray.

Cooper was using a large hand-held magnifier to examine the tooth. He was not surprised that his first assumptions came true. The tooth was still unidentified, but it was clearly a living shark tooth, showing signs of tooth erosion and large pitting. Cooper examined it closer with a periodontal probe.

The tooth still had its shape but there was a huge cavity along the top of the transverse notch down into the root. Closer inspection showed severe decay and a small pocket. This pocket interested him because it looked like it held some tissue. With luck, it would be a sample from the shark, and not one of its victims.

He removed the small half centimeter piece of tissue and placed it onto a slide. He slid it under his microscope, adjusted the dual eyepieces for focus, and looked at the monitor screen mounted on the counter beside the scope. What he was looking at was clearly organic in nature; it looked like a piece of gum tissue from the shark's mouth, possibly scraped off when the tooth was embedded in the wreckage of the ship.

"Oh my," whispered Cooper. "Now to find out whom you belong to."

Cooper turned and picked up an extension phone and dialed one-one-four.

"Lab One," came the voice through the handset.

"Who's this?" Cooper said.

"This is Higgins," Charlie Higgins replied.

"It's Matt, Charlie. I want you to come down to Lab Two and bring a carry box. I've got a tissue sample I want you to run through the DNA sequencer."

"Sure, right away Matt. What's it a sample of?"

"You'll have to see it to believe it."

Holy shit.

That was the first thing to come to Charlie's mind when he saw the four-inch shark tooth Cooper had in Lab Two. The second thing was *'What kind of shark did it come from?'*

Cooper gave him a quick rundown of where the tooth was found, as well as the tooth fragments he had put aside.

"I gotta say, this is a bit of a surprise. I didn't think we'd find anything like this," Charlie said. Charlie's Virginia accent came out, as he got more excited about the find.

"So we don't know where it came from, we can't identify it by observation, but we hope we can find its owner by running the tissue you found and getting its DNA?"

"That's the plan," Cooper said. "But I want you to keep it hush-hush for now. Only the Captain, XO and Doctor Shane know about this, and the crewman who found it has been sworn to secrecy."

"Okay, I get it. Lab One was pretty empty when I left so it should be no problem preparing a sample to run through the Thermo Fischer sequencer. It's the best machine we've got for this and I can bring you the 'read' after it's finished sequencing the four bases."

"I have to say," Charlie said, "that tooth has been exposed to something - that decay and overall condition just isn't normal. Hang on."

And with that, Charlie left Lab Two and headed down the hall. While he was gone Cooper took a longer look at the large shark tooth. He had to agree with Charlie. Besides the size of the tooth and its unordinary design, something had been eating away at this tooth, something unknown, something unnatural.

Charlie came back carrying a small yellow box with a black handle. He put on black rubber gauntlet gloves and came over to the lab table and removed a cable-anchored wand from the yellow box.

"What's that?" Cooper asked.

"It will be easier to answer you in a minute," Charlie explained.

He flipped three toggle switches on the box and then waved the probe wand towards the large shark tooth. There was a loud screeching and clicking sound as the probe got closer to the tooth.

"Well, shit."

"What is it Charlie?"

Charlie Higgins looked directly at Cooper with the most serious face he ever made.

"Mister Cooper, this is a Geiger counter. Your tooth is radioactive."

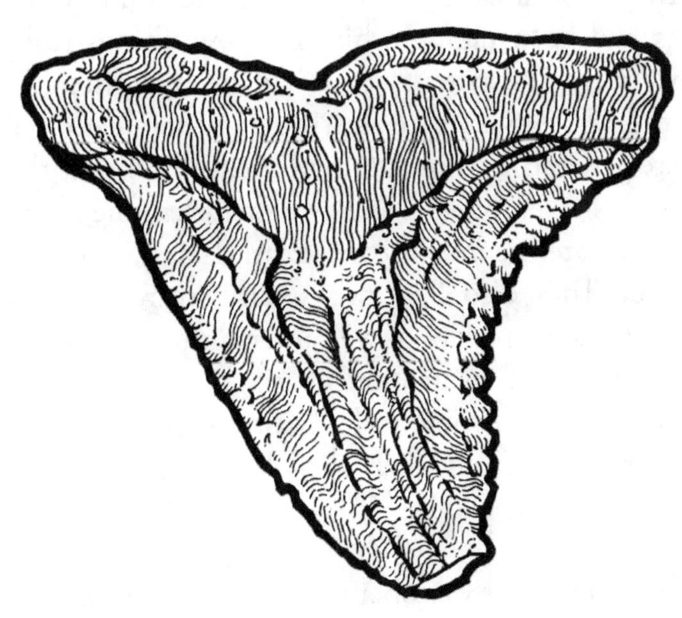

Chapter 6

At the Cooper Institute for Shark Research, Chief Financial Officer Pamela Delaney was drafting an e-mail to Chief Executive Officer Matt Cooper. Cooper had brought her in when he wanted to step away from the financials and become more active in the field. That was 15 years ago and even though Matt Cooper kept in contact with her and the weekly activities of the Institute, she felt it was time for her to give him a bit of a wake-up call on how the Institute was doing during these tough financial times. Matt had used his personal money, mostly from patent licensing, to start the Institute.

With the political environment of the country shifting, the investments had been taking a hit. The only things really keeping CISR afloat were the patents that had been registered from the institute's research. Amazing surgical tools and applications for marine biology were generating annual fees in the millions but the Institute was huge, with 150 employees and two facilities, one here in Florida and a smaller satellite facility on Pearl Island, off the coast of Massachusetts. They also had two small research vessels and the larger *Polaris II*. Docking fees, as well and maintenance, crews and fuel costs were killing them on an annual basis.

Pamela felt it was time to let Mister Cooper know where his money was being spent and where she felt it was time to trim some of the fat.

Pearl Island in late October was not as inviting as it was in July. Bobbi Cooper was standing on the observation porch of the Cooper Institute for Shark Research, Pearl Site, looking at the ocean and seeing a lot of grey. She had been there for two years, only a year after graduating college from the University of New England in Biddeford, Maine. Her dad's cousin, Matt Cooper, ran the Institute and even though she had name notoriety, she got her position all on her own.

She'd met Matt a few times, even worked alongside him on a small excursion, but they weren't close and she made sure her co-workers at the Pearl site knew that. She was on break, needing to get away from the necropsy lab just for a few minutes to clear her head.

A few spinner dolphins had washed ashore on Wildwood Beach in New Jersey and it was up to her to deduce what caused them to beach themselves, or to find out what killed them. Wildwood is known for its eateries, shops, waterparks, boardwalk, and thrill rides and the last thing the residents and shop owners wanted were three dead dolphins washed up on their fancy beach.

One of Bobbi's tasks during the necropsy was to collect any parasites that were revealed and preserve them for further scientific study. She was able to collect a number of worms, including flukes, tapeworms, roundworms, and thorny-headed worms.

Knowing the identity of those worms is important not only to gain a better understanding of the relationship between the worms and their hosts, but also for understanding the interactions between them.

She'll probably find that the majority of the parasites didn't appear to be causing much harm to the dolphins, but rather seemed to be 'flying under the radar' of the dolphins' immune systems.

She took a sip of her cooling coffee; one good thing about the Institute was the coffee. Uncle Matt took care of his people. She was about to head in when she saw a small vessel coming along the dockside of the building. The Institute was built right onto the hillside and partially over the water. Winter storms had been brutal here and things got a bit wet if you were outside.

Their small research vessel, The *Gilligan*, was heading into the dock. It was a 76-ft twin-screw survey boat that could hold twelve crewmen and when needed, could haul ass at thirteen knots.

Today it held a crew of four and Kris Lyons was captaining it.

Kris Lyons with the curly blonde hair and sweet smile that turned all the other women's hearts, and a few of the men's, a flutter. Bobbi didn't care what the others said, Kris Lyons was a hunk and he knew it, but didn't use it to his advantage. He was a sweet guy and a good seaman so he was at the top of her list for people.

Kris was bringing the *Gilligan* into dock when he saw her from the corner of his eye. He gave her a nod and a quick wave and then overcorrected the steering and kissed the side bumper buoy on the dock. He righted the vessel and brought it in smoothly. He looked up at Bobbi and gave an oops gesture. She threw back her head of red hair and laughed. Kris laughed too, his dimples cutting into his two-day old scruff. He had kind eyes and thick blonde hair, just touching the tops of his ears. Right now it looked a mess from the wind and the water spray, but when he did, he cleaned up well.

Bobbi jogged down from the observation porch to the boat, as Kris was getting ready to disembark.

"Smooth move you've got there," Bobbi said. " I thought we'd be repairing that dock again."

"I have to admit that was not my intention but...."

"But?" Bobbi asked.

"But," Kris answered, "I saw your face and it was like a lighthouse guiding me into port."

"Oh my, Mister Lyons, I do believe you are trying to sweet talk yourself out of an embarrassing moment," Bobbi said mimicking a southern belle twang.

Just then the other three-crew members finished tying off the boat and crossed between Bobbi and Kris.

"Walter, please tell me you got pictures of that bump we just made," Dan Grenier asked.

"Oh yes I did, Dan my boy. They're going to look great when I post them on the staff bulletin board."

"I do believe our Captain Kris might have seen a mermaid," Scoggins said.

"Very funny, you three. Take care with those water samples and get them up to Sylwia for testing," Kris ordered.

"Oh yes Captain."

"Right away Captain."

"*Arrr* me Captain."

And the three comedians headed up to the institute leaving Bobbi and Kris on the dock.

"You're not going to live that one down are you? " Bobbi said, smiling at Kris.

"Nope, not in this lifetime."

They both chuckled and headed towards the institutes dockside entrance.

Chapter 7

"Radioactive? How the hell does a tooth become radioactive?" asked Captain Dobbs.

"I have no idea Cap, but the tests Charlie ran came back as slightly radioactive," replied Cooper.

Cooper, Captain Dobbs, XO Menard and Doctor Shane were once again in the stern conference room. This kind of information was not for the ears of the crew.

"How slight is slight? I've got sixty people aboard this ship and at least a half dozen have touched that tooth, including your self, Mister Cooper. I need to know what the fuck is going on and if my crew is in any danger!"

Matt had never seen Dobbs this mad. For him to openly swear was way out of character.

"Charlie and I ran extensive tests. We're not going to die from radiation poisoning, but I think the shark that lost that tooth is."

"Does that explain the pitting and damage to the tooth that you mentioned earlier, Mister Cooper?" asked Menard.

"I think it does. Charlie saw it right away and the Geiger counter confirmed it. The shark somehow became exposed and is slowly being poisoned. It must be in terrible pain. It also explains the radio message from the Gloria J about a large shark. I'm guessing that the extraordinary size is due to the radiation."

"I'll ask it again; how does a shark become radioactive?" asked Captain Dobbs. "It's not like it swam over to Chernobyl and dined on some tasty nuclear waste. And last time I checked, all of our nuclear subs are accounted for."

"I may have an answer for you, but you have to take it with a grain of salt."

"I'll take the whole goddamn bag if it's enough for me to understand this," replied Dobbs.

"But first - Doctor Shane, did any of your patients exhibit signs of radiation sickness, even minor ones?" Cooper asked.

"No. All of the patients are recuperating. There are no signs of weakness, bleeding or open sores," Shane replied.

"Okay then....think back eight years, what nuclear tragedy did our world experience?"

"Oh shit," replied Menard.

"Give the man a cigar."

Captain Dobbs was confused, "I don't know what you're –"

"Fukushima Daiichi nuclear power plant. The accident happened eight years ago and marine biologists have been finding some oddly mutated fish. Now granted, on a smaller scale, but there have been mutations," Cooper explained.

"There's a chance that our big shark's mother was pregnant when the reactor blew and she was irradiated. She would have probably died shortly after from exposure, but she might have given birth to our problem shark. The radiation could have gone right into the embryo's egg sack, and the pup drank it up. After eight years of growing and mutating the radiation is now killing it."

A knock on the conference room broke the tension. Doctor Charlie Higgins stood there looking very happy with himself. Cooper waved him into the conference room.

"Hey Charlie, this is a private meeting –"

"I understand Matt, but I figured out what kind of shark the tooth came from."

"The DNA 'read' came back." Cooper said, looking excited.

"It did," Charlie confirmed. "Our radioactive sick shark is a snaggletooth shark. The sequencer gave me clean reads from the bases and our database confirmed snaggletooth."

"But? I can hear the 'but' in your voice Charlie. Spill it," Cooper demanded.

"Excuse my French, Doctor Shane, but this shark is all fucked up. It's got gaps in its DNA strands and there are extra chromosomes kicking around that don't make sense. I'm surprised it's still alive."

"Thanks Charlie. Head on back to Lab One and start running tests on the tooth fragments we found. I want to know if any of them trigger the Geiger counter. See if you can pull any tissue samples from them for analysis," Cooper asked.

Charlie turned and headed out of the conference room. Captain Dobbs asked the question everyone had wanted to ask.

"What the hell do we do now? I've got seven injured crewmen from a sunken fishing boat. A freaking radioactive shark's tooth and no answers to any of my questions!" exclaimed Dobbs.

"A snaggletooth makes sense. They're very rare. The waters off of Japan fit into their territory," answered Cooper.

"Well just great, we know what kind of shark it is. But I still need answers," replied Dobbs.

"I can help you get some of those answers, Captain Dobbs," offered Shane. "One of the crewmen from the wreck is up for questioning. But I warn you, do not get him too excited. He's got a concussion and we're watching him per our protocols."

"Finally, some good friggin' news. Set it up, Doc. We'll meet you down in sickbay in 30 minutes."

"All right." And with that, Doctor Shane left to arrange the questioning.

Dobbs turned and said, "Okay Cooper, the shit is hitting the fan. We're hopefully going to get some of the answers we need. What I need from you is how screwed up is this shark, why is it swimming with other sharks and where the fuck is it?"

"I'll touch base with Doctor Higgins and get you some answers before our meeting with the crew member," Cooper answered.

"XO, get me a rundown on our crew. Open your ears and let me know the mood. I also want a breakdown of daily activities. Get that Geiger counter from Higgins and get me readings on that shit we took onboard from the Gloria J. I want to know if any of it is radioactive, and if it is, notify me PDQ. I also want you to check out anyone who might have touched the tooth or the debris. I'm going up to the bridge to see when we arrive in Brisbane. I'll see you both in thirty.

"Yes sir, Captain Dobbs," answered XO Menard.

After Captain Dobbs left the room, Steve turned to Cooper.

"A big, radioactive shark. That's a new one."

"No shit," answered Cooper.

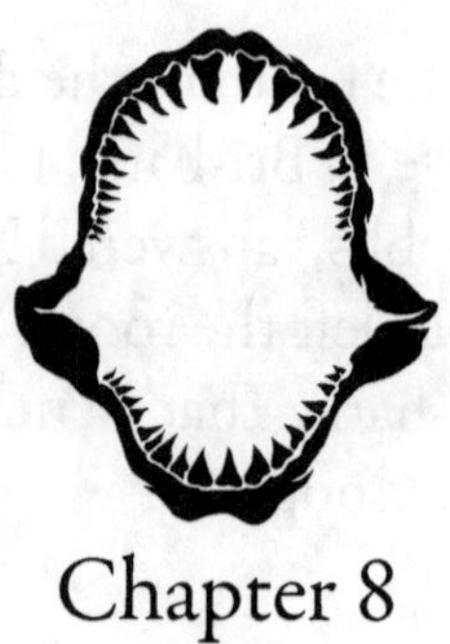

Chapter 8

The giant shark swam through the waters off the coast of Australia. The shark, a male, missed the warmer waters of Japan, but now that he was full size, he had to establish his territory. He had started his life in his mother's placenta with three other littermates; two sisters and a brother. He wasn't the biggest pup, the oldest female was, but he had the more voracious appetite. They constantly attacked each other, causing his eye damage. At five and a half feet long, his mother was above average for a female snaggletooth shark. Months ago she had found herself pinned underneath a much larger male, his claspers searching out her cloaca and impregnating her eggs. Afterwards, the male left her to gestate the eggs until they hatched inside of her.

She hunted as much as she could, eating everything that came across her path, from small fish, to other sharks. She occasionally went close to the surface and snagged seabirds at rest upon a placid sea. After the nuclear reactor explosion and the all around turmoil onshore, the ocean became much warmer, something she did not like, but she was in familiar waters. The prey she had eaten tasted funny to her. All of her pups had been exposed to the leaking radiation, which had flowed into their yolk sacs, and then into their blood, nourishing them. When the Fukushima reactor exploded, she had been three months pregnant with her litter. When she gave birth five months later, she was barely alive, the radiation having ravaged her body, and mutated her litter.

The giant shark's birth was violent, filled with sharp muscle contractions and pain. His expulsion from the world he had lived in for eight months was shocking. At the time of his birth, it was only he and his sister left. They had eaten their siblings in the need to survive. His sister tried eating him on numerous occasions, but he had grown steadily larger until he was twice her size. Their mother, in the throes of birthing, had lost her appetite. This was something nature had wired into her brain, giving her litter a chance to live.

His sister was born first, sliding from the birth canal and escaping into the Pacific Ocean. He was enormous, almost two thirds of what their mother measured. Emerging from the birth canal, he found himself getting stuck due to his large size. He thrashed and tore at his mother until he was finally free. His instinct was to swim away as fast as possible, but instead he stopped and circled his mother. She was bleeding badly and was starting to sink towards the bottom. Pain and blood loss was making her weak and without an air bladder, like other fish, she would drift and drown. He had no pity. Mercy was not hard-wired into him, but there was something special about him. He felt his mother's pain and agony and he knew she was dying.

The newly born shark flicked his tail and picked up speed. His sensitive nose and ampullae picked up his mothers electrical current and blood trail. He swam faster and closed in on her. He did not know good from bad. All he knew was that he had to feed to keep swimming and swim to breath. He charged his mother and bit down on her head, crushing her skull and brain with his powerful jaws. A second bite crushed her spinal cord, paralyzing her. She coughed out a cloud of blood from her mouth and gills. This drove him wilder. He began to rip chunks of flesh from her back and side, chewing and swallowing the pieces, saving it to digest later. The blood ran into his nose and across his gills, driving his mind into a frenzy. Red washed over his simple brain. Impulses began to explode, causing his heart to race, driving his senses to race to new levels, new reaches.

Once he had his fill of his mother's flesh, he looked around for other prey. He saw only small feeder fish, so he turned to where his sister had swam off. He smelled her embryonic fluids and saw the trail she left. He left his mother to die and picked up speed in search of sis. It was time he gave her payback for his damaged eye.

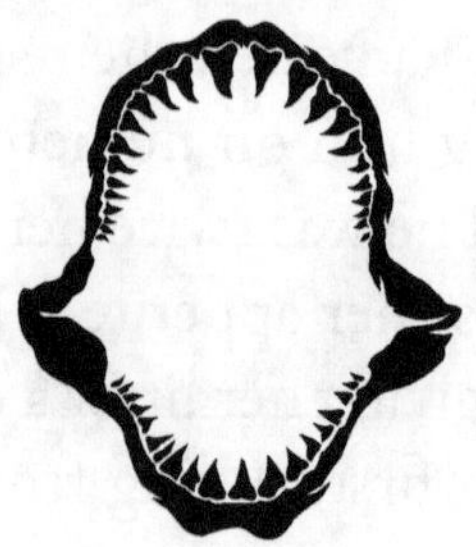

The two pygmy blue whales that the giant shark had attacked and devoured were older and moved slower than the rest of the pod. They were at the rear of the group, so taking them was easy. He would have rather had one of the larger males; the flesh and oils would have revitalized his energy levels. Even the virgin flesh of a few calves would have been good, but he was not feeling at all right. His skin felt wrong, and he occasionally experienced a burning along his lateral line. Taking the two older whales had been the easiest option.

He was now two years old, thirty-five feet in length and close to three tons in weight. He had no enemies swimming these waters, except for the occasional sperm whale or giant squid. As he cruised off the coast of southern Asia, he picked up a few sharks as companions. The makos and tigers saw that the larger shark was able to get bigger and better prey, and what he left behind, kept their appetites satisfied. A few of the tigers tried to move in on the giant shark, but a few quick snaps and body bumps, put them in their place.

He knew he was different from these sharks, and not just because of his size. He felt more *aware* of these sharks and found that he could sway their actions. When they had come across a large school of cod and he wished the tigers to come at the cod from the opposite side, they did. He and the makos simply awaited their arrival, and easily decimated the school. Soon after, a few larger, aggressive shark species like hammerheads and great whites joined them. Wherever the deadly herd moved, smaller fish cleared out of their way.

Chapter 9

Captain Dobbs walked onto his bridge and the silence was deafening. He sat in his Captain's chair and started barking.

"Navigator - ETA to Brisbane?"

The navigator, Burns, jumped with a start, "Thirty-seven minutes sir."

"Amenta, what's the chatter?"

"All quiet, Captain. Brisbane port will have ambulances waiting for us at the dock. The harbor master is going to want a report on the accident and rescue."

"Let the harbor master know that my XO will get him the rescue report and that the deck boss of the Gloria J will get him the accident report once he's settled into the hospital."

"Sir, it sounded like he wanted the paperwork once we docked –"

"Tell him he'll get it when he gets it and when we hit Brisbane, we're pulling a turn and burn and heading back out to sea."

"Aye sir."

"Amenta, any buzz about... sharks?"

The bridge of the *Polaris II* became deathly quiet. The crew was waiting for this answer.

"Sir," Amenta responded, "indirect chatter has two small fishing boats reporting attacks, but with no fatalities...".

"And?"

"There's a small craft watch for a private yacht that sailed out of Brisbane three days ago and was due to check in, but so far no contact."

Captain Dobbs spun his chair around and dead-eyed Amenta.

"How many people are aboard the yacht?"

"Five total....including three children."

"Oh sweet Jesus."

Chapter 10

James Rodgers sat near the bow of his family's luxury super yacht. He had no interest in learning about how to sail or sightsee, he just wanted to enjoy the fresh air, the sunshine, and his illustrated book about sharks.

The family had left their home in Sydney, Australia a week ago and set sail from the docks in Little Bay. They had planned to be away for a month sailing to Auckland, New Zealand, to visit family and stay at one of his dad's seaside resorts.

The Rodgers family was a pioneer in building seaside communities and setting up beautiful resorts for the incredibly wealthy. James' great grandfather started out digging ditches and working during the housing boom of the 1890's. Commercial growth blew up in Auckland, and every capable man who could swing a hammer and plow a shovel was hired to work on the construction sites.

Over the decades, the family expanded their resort locations all along the eastern shore of New Zealand. They then decided they wanted to test the waters of Australia. Three large resorts had been built in Melbourne, Adelaide and Perth, becoming massive moneymakers.

This secured the Rodgers family for the rest of their lives. Gordon Rodgers, James' father, did not want to leave college with his business degree and become an instant Vice President with the company. He wanted to start at the bottom and work his way up to the top, and that is precisely what he did.

Gordon eventually became president of Rodgers Resorts and helped grow the business and stay on top of every consumer's changing needs. He worked hard, loved his family and decided to take everyone away for a long holiday.

The Rodgers family was enjoying the trip, not always an easy thing, with three children all under the age of nine.

They set sail on their Oyster 595, 60-foot sailing yacht. This was a lower class super yacht, but nonetheless an extraordinary vessel. The *Jumping Janet* could sleep nine people with its one master bedroom and three regular bedrooms. It also had couches that could be converted into sleepers, to accommodate more guests.

Nine-years old James enjoyed being out at sea, and really loved reading about ocean life. His latest favorite book was Sharks of the World by Doctor Matthew Cooper. He knew Cooper was a big thing in the shark world, and had seen him quite a few times on television during "Shark Week." He was always very excited when he saw a new shark book on the shelves at Goldens Corner Books.

Six-years old Julia was a pixie. She was truly adorable and mischievous. She adored her mother and father, ignored her older brother, since he would not play with her, and loved to cuddle with her younger brother Jaxon.

He was the baby of the family at three years old. He was full of innocent energy and learned his way around the boat very quickly. All three children loved sailing and never had any problem with seasickness.

James was sitting with the big hardcover book on his lap. His light brown hair was blowing in the breeze, and his blue windbreaker was keeping him warm. He was flipping through the pages and came to the basking shark. He was excited to learn about such a strange shark, and the illustrations by Robert Eggleton were wonderful. Looking up from his book, he saw some fins off the starboard side of the boat. He sheltered his eyes with his hand to see better, and counted four black fins in the distance.

"Hey dad, look out there," he yelled back to his father, pointing.

"What do you see, Jim?"

"Fins. Looks like sharks."

Gordon Rodgers stood up from his seat at the pilot's station and looked out to where his son had pointed. He was tall, with a bit of a pear shape. His baseball cap was tucked down tight, keeping the sun out of his eyes, protecting his balding head from sunburn. The sun's glare was obscuring his sight, so he reached down and grabbed his binoculars. He set the boat on autopilot and looked to the water.

It took him a few seconds to focus where James pointed, and then he saw the fins. He couldn't tell what species of shark was out there, but he decided to keep an eye on them.

"What do you think Jim? Great whites? Tigers?"

"I don't know dad, but look, there are more rising. They're getting closer."

Down below, Gordon's wife Janet yelled up to them.

"Honey, what's going on?"

"There are a some sharks out here, and they're headed our way."

Janet Rodgers came halfway up the stairs from the galley. She looked over the rail and squinted to see what got both of her guys all excited.

"I don't see anything."

"Out there, at about 2:00," Gordon answered, using his arm to point out the fins.

Janet used her hands to shade her eyes and looked out where Gordon was pointing. "Oh, I see them. Are you sure they're sharks? Maybe they're dolphins?"

Julia came running up the stairs at the word "dolphin."

"Dolphins? I love dolphins. They're so cute. Can we swim with them?"

Her two blonde ponytails were bouncing in the wind, the look of awe on her face was amazing. She was so full of life.

"Where are they? I can't see them. Daddy let me use your 'noculars."

"It's *binoculars* honey," her mom corrected, "And they're not a toy. They are an adult thing."

"Oh, poop!"

"Julia Elisabeth Rodgers, watch your mouth!" Her mother said.

"Yes, mom."

"Gordon –"

Gordon heard his wife, but was focused on the school of sharks moving in their direction.

"Gordon –"

No answer.

"Gordon!" Janet yelled.

Gordon quickly looked back at his wife with a scowl on his face. "What is it, Janet? Can't you see I'm watching these sharks!?"

"G-G-Gordon....look," said Janet as she weakly pointed behind her husband.

Gordon quickly looked where his wife was pointing. His mouth dropped open in shock. There were at least a dozen fins following in their wake. They were as close as twenty feet away.
Julia looked behind them and also saw the fins.

"Are those more dolphins, mommy?"

Janet pulled her daughter into her arms and said softly, "No honey, I don't think so."

"Dad!" James yelled, "There are more fins out there." He pointed towards the first fins they had seen.

Gordon looked and saw that the number of fins had doubled. They were weaving along, snake-like, in their direction.

Gordon looked to Janet and Julia, and then to James. Where was his youngest?

"Janet, where's Jaxon. Did he come up with you?"

Janet tore her eyes away from the water and looked at him slightly confused. What did he just ask her? And then the words began to make sense.

"He's down below, taking a nap on our bed."

"Okay," Gordon said. "Take Julia down below and I'll get James."

"Dad!"

Gordon looked up after hearing his son's scream.

"James! Are you alright?"

"Dad, look over there!" James was pointing towards the stern.

Gordon looked past his son and was immediately troubled by

what he saw. He turned to Janet and said, "Take her down below and secure yourselves."

"But...what?"

"Do it now!"

Janet scooped up Julia and headed below decks. Gordon watched his wife and daughter go down and then headed forward to his son. He grabbed his binoculars on the way and settled down next to James.

"James, you should go below."

"Dad, I want to see what that is," as he pointed towards the shape coming towards them.

Gordon raised his binoculars and adjusted the focus wheel. What he saw chilled his bones and made him fear for his family's safety. He saw a shark fin coming towards them, but not just any fin. This one was huge. It was still too far away to see any detail but he guessed it was at least four feet in height and creating a wake that rivaled many large boats. The shark was moving fast and he knew he didn't have any time to navigate his boat away from it. He looked around and saw many smaller fins. This wasn't just a school of sharks passing by, this was an attack. Gordon jumped up and grabbed James by the arm.

"*Ow!*" James exclaimed.

"We have to get down below, *right now!*"

"But dad, I want to see –"

"*NO*, James! We are going now!"

Gordon dragged his son to the rear of the *Jumping Janet* and shoved him down the stairs to the cabin area. Wild-eyed, Gordon looked around and saw the sharks starting to circle his boat. The larger fin was almost on top of them. He could hear James crying from down below and he felt awful about it, but he needed to make sure his family was safe. He checked once more that the autopilot was still engaged, and gave one last look around. What he saw sent creeping tingles up his neck and onto the back of his skull.

The large fin was coming abreast of the ship. He looked over the rail to see the largest shark had ever laid eyes on. It was almost as long as his sixty-foot yacht. It was grotesque in its shape and size. As it passed his ship, he saw an entourage of smaller sharks swimming behind it.

Gordon hurried below deck and closed the rear hatch to the living area. The hatch was aluminum, keeping it light and secure. He threw the deadbolt and then turned and slumped against it. He breathed a sigh of relief and then looked at his family. Janet had all three children huddled around her. All of their eyes were like silver dollars, and filled with fear.

"Gordon, what is it?" Janet asked.

"I have to call the Coast Guard."

All three children were crying, making it hard to concentrate, but Gordon went to the small room that housed their radio and sonar units. He sat down at the desk and searched out the Australian Coast Guards frequency.

"Mayday, mayday, mayday. This is the *Jumping Janet*, a sixty-foot sailing yacht. We are one thousand, one hundred and twenty four kilometers off the coast of Sydney, somewhere in the Tasmanian Sea. We are surrounded by a school of sharks and they are becoming more aggressive to our ship. My wife and I have our three young children here, and we are in fear for our lives. We need help as soon as possible. Please send a cruiser or helicopter. We need help!"

Gordon waited for a response and all he heard was static.

"Do you think they heard you?" Janet asked.

Gordon sighed and looked over his shoulder at his family.

" I don't know. I hope so. I think we're in big trouble."

A loud thump on the hull of the ship quieted everyone in the room. Another, louder thump sounded towards the bow. The children screamed, as did Janet. Gordon looked at his wife and the look on her face scared him more than anything he'd ever seen before.

Another, stronger thump sounded on the opposite wall. Gordon looked over and saw a crack on the wall and he thought he saw a trickle of water.

"Gordon, what is that?"

"I - I think the sharks are ramming the boat."

"What do they want?"

"I don't know!"

"Gordon?"

Gordon looked his wife straight in the eye. "I think they want us,"

"Oh my god."

A stronger thump hit the wall. Gordon was sure he could see a large crack forming.

Then water began to spray into the room.

He looked down at his children. They were scared and crying. James reached out and Gordon took him in his arms. He looked up at the wall as it caved in, letting the ocean into the room. Tons of water poured in, knocking them over and across the room. Gordon held onto his son, and wiped water from out of his eyes. He looked across the room and saw a shark's face forcing it's way through the ruptured wall.

He was hoping the water would kill them before the sharks did.

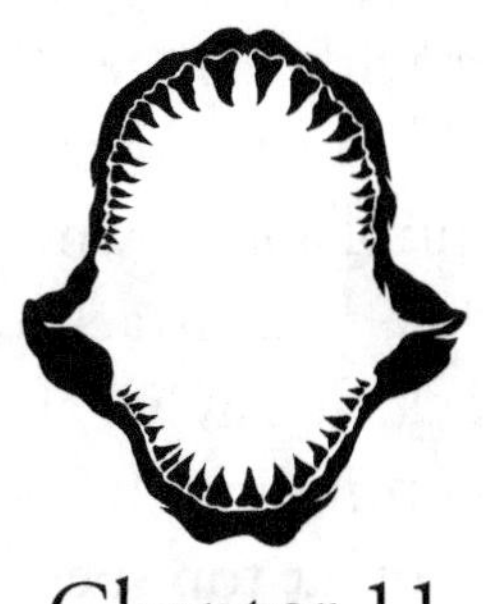

Chapter 11

The herd of sharks continued on their journey through the Coral Sea, taking prey where they could find it. The giant shark was still in the lead when he and a few of the others sensed another alien object half a mile away. Even though the herd fed well on the netted cod, that was fifty miles behind them, and their appetites weren't satiated yet. Some of the larger sharks took off in different directions, looking to encircle this new floating object that was heading towards them. They found with the last attack, that these objects usually contained prey. The giant was not feeling one hundred percent; the breach at the fishing vessel took a lot out of him. He allowed the others to go forward. A couple of the great whites had decided on making a move. One dropped below the giant while the other swam up and paralleled the larger shark. The giant did not seem to notice, but that's what he wanted the whites to think. He had targeted these two as rivals and had been waiting for their attack.

As if a silent signal was sent, the white from below arched upwards and picked up speed. The other white continued to swim along with the giant, coming a bit closer as they continued on. Just as the rising white was about to strike, the giant lowered his pectoral fin and rolled out of the way of the charge. The white continued upward, and the other shark turned towards the giant, as he veered away. Quicker than expected for his size, the giant spun around and charged the white that had been swimming with him. The smaller shark saw the attack and tried to avoid the enormous jaws by veering down, but was too slow. The giant's teeth tore through it's back and sheered off the dorsal fin, filling the water with a huge cloud of blood. The injured shark tried to upright itself, but with its fin missing, and it's spinal cord damaged, it sank uncontrollably downward, into the dark, cold sea.

The great white that had attacked from below had come around to resume the attack. It saw what the giant had done to its accomplice, and debated continuing the attack. The giant shark saw this and charged him head-on at top speed. The giant wasn't feeling any pain now as the excitement of the hunt and adrenaline surged through his system. He was on the white in seconds. He went for a head attack and brought his huge set of jaws and seventy-five teeth into play. His mouth encircled the white's head up to its gills slits, and he slammed his jaws shut. Jaws with irregular, pointed lower teeth impaled the whites jaw while the knife like uppers stabbed into the whites head, crushing the its skull. Blood billowed into the water as the giant thrashed his head and jaws, sawing into the whites flesh. He ripped the other shark's head away, decapitating it. He crushed the head in his jaws, over and over, putting an end to the hostile takeover.

The few remaining sharks that were around him began to swim towards the rest of the herd. They knew who was the dominant force here. The giant followed, sensing the attack on the object that they found earlier. He rose towards the surface, his four-foot dorsal fin announcing his arrival.

Chapter 12

To: bcooper@cisr.com
From: mcooper@cisr.com

Subject: Shark test results

Hi Bobbi,

I hope you're well. How is Pearl? I know, Pearl Island in October sucks, sorry.

We've run into something amazing here off of Brisbane and I wanted you to take a look at these test results that Doctor Charlie Higgins ran. You are the best marine pathologist I know and I would appreciate your opinion. We have our own theories, but I want your open-minded viewpoint.

Thanks,
Matt

P.S., please say hello to everyone there for me.

Doctor Matthew Cooper
Cooper Institute for Shark Research
Miami, FL

Brisbane_shark_sample_test.xls

Chapter 13

Doctor Helen Shane's office was not small, but once you added Captain Dobbs, Matt Cooper, XO Menard and the patient from the Gloria J., things became tight so Menard offered to stand while Shane had a couple extra chairs brought in.

"Gentlemen, this is Max Christy, the deck boss from the wrecked ship and he's agreed to answer your questions. But remember what I told you about his condition, take things slow and easy or this discussion is over," Shane explained.

The men agreed to let Cooper speak with the sailor, so he began the questioning.

"Hi Max, my name is Matt Cooper. How are you doing? We are concerned with your fellow crewmembers and we want you to know that all of them are getting the best medical attention possible. We're heading into Brisbane where we'll make sure you all go straight to the Royal Brisbane hospital for further treatment.

"Max, I know you've spent seven years at sea and I'm sure you've seen some weird shit, but we need to know what happened to the Gloria J. Are you up to telling us?"

Max Christy was in his early thirties, average build with dark sandy hair and strong blue eyes. He had a hospital dressing around his head and a large gauze pad above his left ear where he took a hit during the accident. It didn't require stitches, but he'd had some blood loss.

"I'm glad to hear my guys are okay," Max stated. "Doctor Shane told me about Henry's leg. That's a tough break for a young kid.

"I'll tell you what I can. My memory is a bit foggy because of the shot to my head."

Matt said, "Go on take your time."

Max continued. "We had been out for four days, fishing was

good and we were hauling back when we saw the sharks."

Everyone except Max looked at each other. Here was the first-hand corroboration they were looking for.

"Now keep in mind, we see sharks all the time. Shit, it's Australia, so we see them with every haul back, but this was different. We were hauling the trawl in from the stern when we started seeing different kinds of sharks taking bites out of our catch. Sometimes we'd see great whites or some blues but this was a lot of different sharks. Most of the deck crew was gathered near the stern watching the frenzy. I was amidships at the hauler when we started feeling hits to the boat. God-damn sharks were attacking the boat!"

"Max, I want you to take a deep breath, try to calm down," interrupted Doctor Shane.

"If you could keep going Max, that would be great," Cooper added.

Cooper caught the side-eye Shane threw at him, but they were so very close to getting the answers they needed.

"I yelled to my guys to get away from the rail. I'll be honest I had never seen this kind of feeding frenzy before. There must have been a hundred sharks tearing apart our net. Fourteen hundred kilos of herring going down their gullets.

The sea was choppy and there was spray all over the deck. I heard a couple of my guys yelling and then I heard them screaming. I couldn't see what was going on real well, but what I did see was the biggest goddamn shark I ever saw leaping out of the water and land-ing across our net. He must have weighed eighteen thousand kilos, probably nine meters in length. He was an ugly prick with messed up teeth, a white-eye and skin that looked wrong. It was all splotchy.

"Anyway," Max continued, "it landed right on our net. That extra weight brought the stern right down into the water and that's how I lost most of my guys. They went in the water and the sharks went to town on them. The big one kind of lays on the trawl net, like he's taking a nap, and then slithers off it, back into the ocean as we started to take on water."

Max showed signs of exhaustion, but he kept going.

"With the stern below water, the bow was pointing up to the sky. I heard yelling from below decks, it sounded like the engine room was flooding. We had three guys down there. They didn't have a chance."

"Max, if you need to stop, I'll put an end to this meeting," interrupted Doctor Shane.

"I'm okay Doc, I'm tired but my head is still clear.

"Anyways," Max continued, "I was able to get back into the prep room and hang on while we sank. The sharks eating my guys all over the place, it was the worst thing I ever saw. The lower decks were filling with water, we tipped to the starboard and started to roll over.

"Next thing I know we're in the water and when the boat went belly up we had a couple minutes to get ourselves onto the hull and grab anyone we could. I'm guessing the Captain and the radioman in the wheelhouse didn't make it."

"And then we showed up," declared Captain Dobbs.

"That you did Cap, and we greatly appreciated it."

"Max, I want to thank you for sitting with us. I'm sure it was hard to have to relive all that horror, but you gave us some much needed answers," Cooper said.

"And we should be pulling into Brisbane Harbor any minute so we'll leave you alone to get your guys and get ready to head to the hospital," said Dobbs.

Everyone rose to leave and then Max turned to Doctor Shane and gave her a gentle hug.

"Thanks Doc for saving my men. We'll always remember you."

"Take care Max, I'll follow up with Royal Brisbane and make sure all of your treatment records are sent over. Bye."

Max left Doctor Shane's office and headed to the sickbay.

"Gentlemen and lady, let's get these guys into Brisbane. Then we figure out what our next course of action is," ordered Dobbs.

Chapter 14

The giant always took the lead. As this unique, unnatural shiver of sharks entered the waters off of eastern Australia, the giant smelled blood in the water. Distressed fish were somewhere up ahead. He felt their fear and anxiety. They were all in one large group at the surface, near a larger object. It smelled different, not like prey. Something he had only sensed from great distances. It smelled of bitter oils and pungent fuels. Baitfish surrounded it – their next target. He went ahead, keeping below the surface, swimming along with the larger object, occasionally bumping it, and trying to get a feel of what it was. He knew it was not food; its hard surface was smooth in some areas, and covered with rough barnacles on others. It moved slowly, fighting its way through choppy seas. He decided the time to attack was now.

The sharks began to circle the object, bumping it, coming in for quick attacks, trying to damage it. Some of the makos started to tear at the fish, mostly cod, trapped within a large net. The cords of netting snapped against the teeth of the sharks, leaving the cod to spill out into the waiting mouths of the others. The herd's collective blood began to boil. A feeding frenzy began. Feeding was all that mattered.

The giant fed on the cod that tried to escape. He was too fast for them, but was growing impatient. He wanted more and he wanted it now.

The giant dove down to a hundred feet, flipped his tail and started upward, gaining speed as he rose. Cod steered clear of the savage rocket. The other sharks paused and watched as their leader rose past them and left the water. Breaching the surface, traveling fifty feet into the air, he felt sharp pains in his liver and along his lateral line as he came down. He didn't know what was causing the pain, but it made him veer sideways and come down on the net full of fish. His additional weight submerged the net and made the large alien object drop its rear and start to take on water. The giant lay on the net for a few more seconds while the pain subsided, and then slowly rolled off the net, back into the water. He had no more appetite. He needed to get away from the others and rest. The giant left behind his herd of frenzied killers, letting them devour the rest of the cod, and whatever they could find on the strange object.

Chapter 15

The ambulances were waiting at the wharf when the *Polaris II* docked at Bay 6. All the patients were able to get to the ambulances except for Henry Wilson; he had to be stretchered off the boat. Once the patients were offloaded, crewmembers jumped to it, getting on extra supplies and sending off packages headed either to the Pearl site or to the home base in Florida. The fuel tanks were topped off and the *Polaris II* headed back out to sea, fourteen hours later.

Dobbs, Cooper and Menard met on the observation deck just off the bridge. The Captain liked to keep an eye on the departure of his boat from any seaport. It was a habit he had always had; he wanted to make sure all went well with his comings and goings from port. He'd seen his share of accidents caused by sloppy crew work and lazy command decisions.

"What's on your mind, Captain?" asked Cooper.

"After looking at the reports of the accident, Doctor Shane's analysis and your notes Matt, I'm all for heading back out to the Coral Sea to see if we can find this big shark and his herd. I want to make sure that no one else gets hurt or killed. Thoughts, gentlemen?"

"Captain," said Menard, "I've gone over all the wreckage we took onboard and we didn't find anything else radioactive. I checked out the crewmembers that had come in contact with the debris and the tooth and they're all clean. I've also spoken to members of the crew and they are all in for hunting down this big shithead shark and taking him and his buddies down."

"Now hold on Menard," interrupted Cooper. "This is a major biological find, something the Institute was created for, and I think we can handle it. This shark needs to be found and studied, not killed on sight. We need to find out why it got so big, how much radiation it absorbed, and why these other sharks follow it. Even if we find it dead, it will be months of work until we find out all of these answers, but it's answers we need. Who knows what other marine animals are out there that have been affected by the radiation from Fukushima.

"Captain," Cooper turned and pleaded, "we gotta find this shark. My guys in the lab are trying to figure a way to track it based on its radiation levels. I've got Markowski and Amenta working together on satellite imaging to see if they can pinpoint if it was Fukushima where this originated."

"Hmmm...," murmured Dobbs. "Fellas, I can see both your positions. XO, I want you to speak to the crew, get them onboard a 'search and study plan', but keep them ready for any kind of defensive action that might be needed. Cooper, get your lab guys going on finding this shark and going over the samples. Pull Johnson from Engineering to help Amenta and Markowski.

"I want to know where this shark came from and where it is now. A lot of the recent attacks have happened near the Coral Sea so that's where we are headed."

"Aye sir," replied Menard as he exited, leaving the two older men at the rail.

"Coop, deep in my heart I want to see that shark hanging by it's tail from my crane, but I also know you own this boat and sign my check so I'm compromising here, you read me?"

"I gotcha, Cap. You have a responsibility to your crew and the boat and the last thing you want is a bunch of lab rats in your way, but this is some important shit here. We'll get you the results you're looking for," answered Cooper.

"Thanks, Matt," responded Dobbs.

Chapter 16

To: mcooper@cisr.com
From: bcooper@cisr.com

Subject: re: Shark test results

Hello Matt,
I've received your document and spent some time going over Higgins' results. This is amazing! What the hell have you found out there? I've looked at the tissue and DNA report and I concur that this snaggle-tooth shark has some huge gaps and damage to its DNA structure. Judging by its radioactivity levels and estimated age, I am guess-timating that it's got a couple of months left to live, maybe 6 at the most. It's got to be in constant pain. Eventually it's going to suffer from organ failure and probably complete sensory deprivation. If none of these kill it, its motor functions will fail and it will stop swimming and drown.
I wish I were out there to take live tissue samples. If you capture it, send me its corpse. I could write a dozen papers on what I might find.
Everything is good here, cold, rainy, windy. Fall on a lovely island. Wish you were here, LOL.

Talk soon,
Bobbi
Doctor Roberta Cooper
Cooper Institute for Shark Research
Pearl Island, MA

Chapter 17

Cooper was taking a few minutes rest in his stateroom to catch up on e-mails and messages. Bobbi had responded to his e-mail and she was very excited about their find. Matt thought if she was here and had seen the destruction of the Gloria J, maybe she would not be so excited to be onboard. He wrote back and promised to keep her updated on their progress. He'd been on the run since early morning, and he needed to take a nap. He lay down on his bed, lowered the lights and quickly fell asleep.

The buzzer rang like an irritating gnat. It pierced Cooper's skull and as his mind cleared and he awoke. He was pissed.

"Hold your horses, I'm coming!" he yelled.

He opened the door to his stateroom and screamed out, "This had better be damn good!"

Paper Markowski and Jon Johnson from Engineering were standing in front of his door with shocked expressions on their faces.

"Well shit, I can stay in my office and get yelled at," Johnson quietly retorted.

"I'm sorry fellas, I was finally asleep," Cooper answered sheepishly. "What can I do for you?"

Neither man answered as fast as Cooper would have liked. Both seemed to be in a bit of shock.

"Paper, speak up, what have you got?"

The bearded giant cleared his throat. "I think we found the routethe shark followed. You were right about Japan."

"Come in boys, let's not talk in the hallway."

The three men sat down at a small table in the corner of Cooper's stateroom. He did not know Johnson well; he was one of Menard's hires, but came highly recommended. He was another tall one, well over six feet with a medium build. He had short, light brown hair and a face full of beard stubble. He wore the casual uniform of chinos and company branded polo shirt that most of the crewmembers favored. Paper still had on his lab coat and under that Cooper saw the company polo.

Paper said, "We went through satellite imagery found on the company's server. By keying in a search query, we found that our big shark did not show up visually until five years ago. By tracking possible paths he might have taken, the paths led back to Northern Japan."

Paper opened his tablet and launched a slideshow. "We also searched using different parameters at the time of the nuclear accident and we have high-resolution satellite imagery of the radioactive bloom. Now we let things die down for eighteen months, because the whole region is hot as hell, and we see this -"

Paper pointed to a red dot off the coast of Japan.

"A radioactive bloom approximately five miles off the coast of Katsuura and if we follow it over a period of months." His finger moved along a path. "And it continues down the Asian coast, hangs around the Philippines for a while - looks like it stakes a claim on the western shore of Papua New Guinea - and then for some reason it heads South East to the Coral Sea."

"That's great, Paper but are you sure?" asked Cooper.

Paper nodded his head. "Absolutely. JJ and I wrote an algorithm to search various current movements and to look for radioactive anomalies. We chewed up a few terabytes in running the program and got these readings."

Johnson spoke up. "Once we found our hot target and were able define it to the search, it didn't take long for our program to track it, but it took some tweaking to keep it on task."

Cooper asked, "Any idea where the shark is now?"

"Judging by our results, he's still hanging around the Coral Sea," Paper answered.

"And the other sharks?" Cooper asked.

"No way to tell," said Johnson. "If they're not radioactive our program can't follow them. If any of them are tagged, we could pick up their satellite signal if it's still sending. If any of them are fitted with a Pop Up Satellite Archival tag, then we'll get more specific data."

"Wow," Paper sarcastically said.

"I told you I'm not just a pretty face." Johnson replied.

"That's all good but let's get back on to the shark subject. How long do you think it will take to find any of these tagged sharks?" Cooper asked.

"Really?" Johnson asked. "You know more about sharks than anyone, and you know there are close to a billion sharks in the oceans, maybe 400 species. The chances of our finding a couple of tagged sharks is slim and almost none."

"You said 'almost'".

"Matt, you hired us for our abilities. I'm not going to rule out our being able to find your shark buddies, but I wouldn't get your hopes up."

"Johnson, Markowski, find me a tagged shark in the Coral Sea. Think of it as one of the most important things you'll ever do. If you need help, Captain Dobbs offered Amenta's assistance," Cooper replied.

"And boys," Matt said, "Find me our shark and I'll personally write you both a fat bonus check."

"That's what I'm talking about!" Johnson exclaimed.

Charlie Higgins was in Research Lab 2 working on the shark tooth found in the wreckage of the Gloria J when Doctor Himari Kohi came in and sat next to him.

"Hello Himari," Charlie said. "How are things in Lab One?"

"A bit quiet, Charlie. Your tooth has taken precedence over much of the research onboard. With us sailing back to the Coral Sea, we probably won't be tagging any sharks. I've got a week's worth of scheduling going to waste!"

Charlie had seen Himari irritated before, even slightly mad, but never this angry.

"This is a big deal and lives have been lost. For now finding this radioactive shark and its herd has been moved up the list.

Besides, Captain Dobbs is not letting anyone in or near the water. He wants to find this shark and let us examine it, or Menard and his goons will kill it and leave us with nothing."

Himari leaned in against Charlie's shoulder. She was hoping for an uneventful six months onboard doing research. Tagging sharks, tracking their migration and then afterwards telling her parents about her relationship with Charlie. She truly loved this awkward and funny man from West Virginia and wanted to be his wife. Her parents were traditional Japanese and believed that she should marry a Japanese man, not a *Shiroi Amerikahito,* or "white American". Himari grew up under their rule and she obeyed their traditions. But once she went to the Florida Institute of Technology and found out what life was like away from her family, she blossomed into a liberated woman who was also one of the pre-eminent marine biologists in the country.

"I understand that, but we're all walking into each other in Lab One. Can I help you here?"

Charlie said, "Let me ask Cooper about that, I don't think it will be a problem. In fact, you could help me with the imaging of the tooth and that will get us more answers, faster."

"Do you think if we don't find the shark, Captain Dobbs will allow us to continue the tagging?"

"I don't know, but Cooper can ask for us. I'd like nothing more than to be tagging sharks. It would give me the chance to streamline the process and make sure the shark cradle is working at one hundred percent. Plus, I like seeing you in your sleek wet suit," Charlie added. He gave Himari a playful smile. Her responding smile brightened up the room, and she felt comforted.

Chapter 18

The *Polaris II* arrived in the Coral Sea under calm seas and warm temperatures. All hands were on the ready and tension was high. Cooper and Higgins had no new results from the tooth. Teeth shards showed that different species of sharks were involved, but none of them were radioactive.

Menard's people went back through the wreckage debris looking for more tissue samples but found nothing. The Geiger counter never triggered any new readings.

Amenta, Johnson and Markowski had continued tracking the radiation signature that never moved out of the Coral Sea. The deepest spot in the sea is 30,000 feet, leaving the big shark many places to hide, diminishing the satellite readings. If it moved out into shallower waters, they would see it. Locating previously tagged sharks had been a huge disappointment. Doctor Higgins and his staff had tagged at least 14 sharks in the Coral Sea, but none had been found in the area.

The Australian Maritime Border Command had made sure that all commercial and private boats were kept out of the area. They continued to search for the private yacht that had turned up missing, but no one ever expected to see it. The Border Command and the Volunteer Coast Guard stayed on stand-by in case the *Polaris II* needed any assistance in their search for the snaggletooth shark and herd. Any requests from news agencies had been turned down and all private aircraft and helicopters were advised to stay out of the area. This freed up Cooper and the *Polaris II* to search the sea without any interference.

XO Menard came up to Captain Dobbs while he was sitting in his captains chair looking out at the Coral Sea.

"Captain, we have another request from Mister Cooper for

Doctor Higgins to resume shark tagging."

Dobbs replied sternly, "Mister Menard, please inform Mister Cooper and Doctor Higgins that no one is going near the water until I am perfectly certain that everyone will be safe. The *Polaris II* is our prison and our shield and until I am certain, no one gets wet."

Mister Menard continued, "Captain, it's been three days. We've sent out the Zodiac ERB dozens of times and Johnson has done flyover searches with his drones. We haven't seen a big glowing shark nor any other sharks. Heck, we've had the *Polaris II* cruising a grid pattern morning, noon and night and we've got nothing. I think the nerd squad have got it wrong and the sharks aren't here."

Captain Dobbs swung to face XO Menard and leaned forward so only he would hear him. "*We* have not had the *Polaris II* searching these waters, Mister, *I* have. And as Captain of this ship *I* say when we stop searching and when it's safe. Do you understand me?"

Menard snapped to attention. He knew he had overstepped his position but he swallowed it and took his orders.

"Yes, sir," replied Menard. "Is there anything else you need from me sir?"

Captain Dobbs stood up from his chair, still having to slightly look up to his XO.

"Steve, I'm tired. I've been in that chair for three days with no sleep, so bear with me. I want everyone safe, understood?"
Menard said, "Okay, Cap."

And just like that, the tension was gone; the roostering was put aside and the search for the sharks continued.

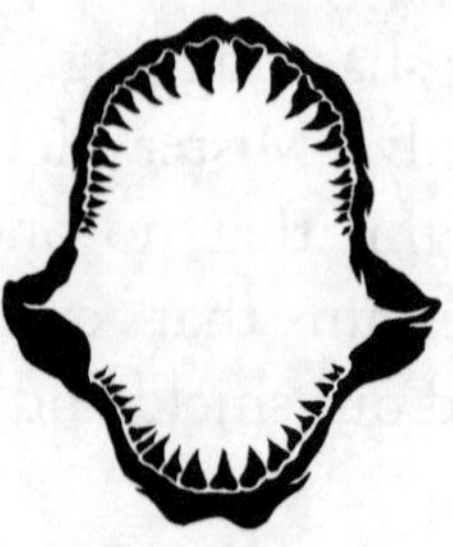

The giant shark and his herd had sensed a much larger intruder into their waters. This one smelt of oil, fuel, discarded waste and blood. They also saw a smaller object moving through the water, circling the larger one. The giant swam below seeing, tasting, smelling, and sensing this larger intruder. The smaller thing was dragging some of their herd towards the other thing. They would be dragged to the rear of its mass, and then would disappear. Shortly, they would reappear and swim away, smelling of something alien.

Chapter 19

Four days went by and still no sign of the sharks. Captain Dobbs was beginning to think they had missed them, so he made the decision to allow Doctors Higgins and Kohi to continue with their research and to tag sharks with satellite beacons. It was a simple process; an ERB driven by three men went fishing with rod and reel until they hooked a shark. They slowly dragged the shark to the *Polaris II*'s shark cradle, attached to the stern.

The cradle could be lowered down three feet below the water's surface. Once the shark was in the open area of the cradle platform, it was raised, stranding the shark on the wooden platform deck. A towel was dropped over the shark's eyes to help eliminate fear - thrashing and high stress levels. Then an industrial hose was forced into the shark's mouth to keep oxygenated water flowing through its gills. Measurements were taken, blood was drawn, and a satellite tag was screwed onto the dorsal fin of the shark causing it no long-term harm. Once the cradle platform was cleared, the hose was withdrawn, the towel removed, and the cradle was lowered into the water.

Most times the shark lethargically swam away. Sometimes a crewmember, usually Higgins, helped the shark off of the platform. The crew and science staff had done it so many times it had become second nature; second nature with the heightened stress level of tagging a dangerous animal.

The day's plan was to tag three sharks; preferably a grey reef, a white tipped reef, and a bronze whaler. All three species had lost huge numbers of population to fishing, therefore green zones, areas closed to fishing, had been set up to protect them. Tagging these sharks would help track migration paths. Satellite imagery would show where in the Coral Sea, these sharks were located.

Gathered at the stern rail were Doctor Higgins and Kohi, Cooper, XO Menard, Markowski and engineer Johnson. In addition were Doctor Abigail Bissette, a marine biologist from Canada who had flown down for this tagging trip, and a handful of crew and assistants. Doctor Shane had sent up a small medical team, just in case there were any injuries. Driving the chase boat were crewmembers Ron Veitch, Tom Williamson and Al Yeates. All had been out fishing together, and had made a good team.

"*Polaris II* to *Rover*, Higgins here, come in *Rover*," Higgins said into his radio.

"*Rover here, Higgins. This is Veitch, I read ya,*" came the reply.

"How does it look out there? What's your location?"

"*We're about a kilometer due South of you, Higgins. There've been some nibbles, but the sharks seem skittish. You certain you want a grey, a white tip and bronzie?*"

"Higgins to Veitch, dead certain. We want one from each of those three species. They're the ones that are taking a huge hit on population."

"*Roger, we'll do our best.*"

Doctor Kohi came up to Higgins's side, "What do you think, shark or no shark?"

"I'm not sure, Himari," Charlie replied. "We usually have no problems hooking a shark. I know we're being very specific this time around, but-"

"*Veitch to Higgins, fish on!*"

"Here we go," Charlie said to Himari. "Great news, Veitch! What have you got on the line?" Charlie said into his walkie-talkie.

"*We've got us a beautiful bronzie! He passed by the boat a few times and then took our bait. Looks to be about three meters, I guess around 200 kilos. We've got him hooked real good, we're going to bring him in.*"

"That's great Veitch, bring him in, we'll be ready!" Higgins responded.

"Okay everyone, you heard the boat. We've got a ten foot bronze whaler coming our way, should be here in about 15 minutes. I'll be on the platform and I want Himari with me. Abigail, I want you to be ready to prepare samples. Mister Cooper, if you want to get wet, you're more than welcome."

"Naw, that's okay. I've done my share of tagging. It's for the young at heart and the more agile," Cooper said.

"Your loss, Matt, this will be a fun one," Higgins added.
The shark tagging went without a hitch. The bronze whaler was fairly calm, even on the cradle platform. All the samples, measurements and tag applications went perfectly, and the release was textbook. The shark just wanted to get back in the deep blue sea. Everyone breathed a little easier after the cradle was raised and out of the water.

"Now, that my friends," announced Charlie Higgins, "is how you do a tagging!"

Everyone in attendance cheered and clapped. This was the tension breaker they all needed.

Charlie added. "Now someone get Veitch on the horn and have him get us another shark!"

The crowd went wild, except for Cooper, who was on deck and Dobbs, who watched all of this from monitors on his bridge. Both men were still nervous about anyone being in or near the water.

By the end of a very long day, two bronze whalers and two grey reef sharks were landed, inspected, measured, tagged, and released. Higgins, and especially Himari, wanted to get a white tip reef shark, but that would have to wait for another day. Tonight they would have a fine meal in the galley, maybe drink a little too much wine and beer then get back to it the next day.

"My man, Joey T!" shouted Jon Johnson as he entered the galley, "What have you got for us tonight?"

Joey T., the executive chef aboard the *Polaris II*, looked up from his prep station and waved out to Johnson.

"For you, my friend, nothing but the best roast duck you've ever had, but not with dull orange sauce, no, but with a spicy plum sauce."

"Hot damn, we worked hard today, so bring it on!" he yelled back, rubbing his hands together.

Joey Tortoriello worked a dozen years in restaurants all throughout New England before moving south to Florida, where he caught the eye of Matt Cooper. He had knocked Matt's socks off with an Italian Bolognese sauce that his mother had taught him. Cooper made him an on-the-spot-offer to feed his crew on the *Polaris II*.

Joey T. was a tough looking guy, with average height, short black hair, and sad eyes. Eyes that said he had a lot going on behind them. Before Florida and Cooper, he had been in poor physical health; overweight, on too many medications and worn down by the daily grind. Cooper gave him the chance for a big change and now after increasingly better doctor's reports and a weight loss of one hundred pounds, Joey Tortoriello was a cooking machine.

His staff of five cranked out breakfast, lunch and dinner for some extra hungry crewmembers and scientists. Mealtime was always a delight aboard ship.

Johnson joined Markowski and Amenta after getting his plate heaped with plum sauce duck, Basmati rice and steamed baby bok choy. The three of them had struck up a friendship and meals together had been a lot of laughs.

"So J.J., you guys were down on the deck," stated Amenta. "What was the vibe from the crew? Anyone shitting themselves or was it chill?"

Johnson immediately responded with, "Shitting themselves."

"I gotta agree," replied Paper. "They were trying to put on a good front, especially Higgins, but you could feel the tension. It got better after we had four successful catch and releases."

Amenta added, "Captain Dobbs was white-knuckling his chair every time someone went near the water. He eased up as the day went by, but the bridge was a freaking tomb. No one spoke, we were all on pins and needles waiting for something nasty to happen."

Johnson said, "And we're going to do it all over again tomorrow. Menard has me getting up at the crack of dark thirty to have my drones searching the water for any sharks. He's not taking any chances."

"I wish our satellite searches had turned up something else, but so far no radiation readings," added Paper.

"Let's hope tomorrow is just as successful as today was" Amenta said.

"I agree."

"Same here, fellas," and they all raised their glasses and toasted the coming day.

Chapter 20

Bobbi Cooper looked at herself in her mirror and liked what she saw.

She wasn't the prettiest girl in the room, nor was she the slimmest, but she was happy with how she turned out.

She was average height with broad shoulders, made strong when she competed as a swimmer. Her hair was auburn, picking up blonde highlights, and sometimes looking black at dusk. Tonight she was wearing it down, the ends hitting her shoulders. Most days at work, she wore it pulled back in a ponytail, or up in a bun. It made wearing eye protection and respiratory masks easier.

She had green eyes and heavy brows that she plucked. A straight nose and full lips, and when she smiled, it came from her heart.

Her figure was curvaceous, so she was not a runway twig. She liked to jog when the weather permitted, to keeping her thighs under control.

Kris was picking her up for dinner tonight. They had a nice chat at the Institute before they left, and found they were both craving Chinese food.

Kris suggested Tao's Asian Cuisine on the North-side of the island and Bobbi thought that was a great idea. Tao's was a comfortable, sit-down place. Pearl Island had four Chinese restaurants, with three favoring take-out. Two were good, and one should be shutdown by the Board of Health.

Bobbi was torn on what to wear, but decided on clean blue jeans, and her nice black, soft, cotton sweater. She didn't wear earrings or rings. She liked necklaces, and the one she wore tonight had a half-moon of colorful abalone shell on a simple silver chain.

She stood back, eyed herself again, and declared this a done project.

Her doorbell rang, so she knew Kris was good at being on time.

She walked through her one bedroom apartment. It was a second floor walk-up. Her downstairs landlords, the Moriarty's, were a kind, older couple that adored her. She kept an eye on them and they took care of her.

Her place was tidy with a simple galley kitchen, bathroom, and a combination living room/dining room. She ate a lot of take-out, so her dining table was more like a marine biologists lab. Her laptop, dissection tools and trays, research books and notepads dominated the table.

Bobbi opened the door and Kris Lyons was standing there in a pair of chinos, denim shirt and a light, waterproof jacket.

"Hey you, are you ready to go? Asked Kris.

"You bet. Let me get a jacket. Is it raining out?"

"It's overcast, but just misting, so water-proof would work." Bobbi grabbed her windbreaker and they headed to Tao's.

"Oh my gosh, that is some fine food!"

Bobbi sat back from the table with a huge, satisfied smile on her face. Kris just laughed and matched her smile.

"So you liked it, I guess?" Kris asked.

"So, so good."

Bobbi liked a lot of different foods. Once as a teen, her parents took them out to a dim sum restaurant and her brother Stan dared her to eat barbecued chicken feet. She was never one to back down, so the feet where eaten and determined to be tangy, sweet and a bit chewy.

Her favorite comfort Chinese food was egg foo yung. It was a bit peasant, but the house egg foo yung at Tao's was loaded with all of her favorites.

Kris wasn't adventurous, but he liked spice, so he went with Tao's General Tso's chicken. They were the only restaurant on the island that did not serve it with broccoli. Kris was a meat and potatoes guy, and most things green did not make it to his plate.

"You know it's just a fancy name for a Chinese omelet," Kris said with a smile.

"Ha-ha Mister No-Veggies. One of these days I will order for you, and we'll see how you do."

"So," Kris asked. "Have you heard from your uncle?"

"Wow, nice segue Mister Lyons."

"It's just something that's been on my mind. Everyone at work is talking about a big shark and a fishing boat that was attacked."

"Uncle Matt asked me to keep it to just the marine bio lab, but I guess I can share it with you. Just don't share it with your crew."

"You mean my Stooges? I don't share anything personal with them. You show any sign of weakness and they'll stick it to you. It's all in good immature fun but sometimes it gets carried away, and then I have to play daddy."

Bobbi ate a little bit more of her dinner, and then sipped her hot green tea.

"Uncle Matt said that things are getting scary, and that he has never seen sharks behave like this before. For him to say that means something weird is going on in Australia."

"I'm glad that we're here on good-old boring, Pearl Island."

Bobbi raised her teacup towards Kris, "You can say that again." They toasted each other, and finished their meal.

Pearl Island is a small island off of the southeastern coast of Massachusetts. The easiest access is from Cape Cod. Pearl was not the largest of the States islands, Martha's Vineyard was, but it had a large population and a thriving economy.

At one point the restaurants almost outnumbered the citizens, but that was the 1990's and now the only ones left, were the best ones.

The island was almost 50 miles square. You couldn't walk across it in a timely manner. The lower end of the island was the heaviest populated and getting from one side of Pearltown to the other, took 45 minutes. Both Bobbi and Kris lived downtown, on either side of the tourist section. Both would walk to the Institute every morning from their opposite sides, sometimes seeing each other on the way in. Sometimes arrived at different times, depending on their work schedules.

Kris was on call to the research staff. There were weekly chores, like tending to the *Gilligan*, the Institute's medium sized research vessel. Compared to the *Polaris II*, it was a dingy, but it could hold eight crewmembers, and enough scientific equipment for small excursions. Kris' boat mates, Grenier, Holl, and Scoggins were a rowdy bunch, but when work needed to get done, you could rely on all three.

Kris and his crew also did most of the supply runs for the Institute so they were constantly on the run. The scientists had a habit of forgetting about weekly scheduled runs, and requested special trips. Scoggins liked to bitch about it, but Kris would make time for the science staff.

If the workload was heavy Bobbi was first in and, at most times, last to leave. Her supervisors knew she was the best and the brightest among the staff, and they ignored that her last name was Cooper. She proved herself on her own, not by who birthed her.

Kris Lyons grew up in Wakefield, MA, living next to train tracks on the lower side of the city. He was infatuated with boats from an early age, and made a decision to learn as much as he could about them. Piloting, maintaining, course plotting, he could do it all. After finishing high school, Kris applied to the Navy, but was turned down for two reasons; permanent hearing loss in his left ear and color blindness. The hearing he knew about, and had hoped he could get by with it, but he was surprised by the color blindness. He never knew what he was missing, so he never explored the possibility of it not getting him into the Navy.

Disappointed but not defeated, Kris packed his things and moved to Pearl Island, hoping to work on the docks, or on charter boats. He put in his years and when he saw an ad in the local paper to work for the Institute, he applied, and was made captain of his own boat and crew.

The walk back to Bobbi's apartment was a short one, and the couple held hands the entire time. They both knew there was attraction between them, so they let it grow. Kris walked Bobbi to her door, said goodbye and turned to leave, but she slowly spun him back and kissed him. There was no hesitation, just a bit of surprise. It felt right and they both embraced, adding more kisses to their collection.

Bobbi had let them into her place, hoping for something, but nervous about other things. In the end, Kris spent the night, but neither was ready for sex. It was a night full of conversation, touching, kissing and nothing more.

Chapter 21

The next day, it was Doctor Kohi's turn to run the tagging team. Higgins was with her at the stern, but he wanted Himari to feel more comfortable being the boss and in charge of the crew. A good scientist was only as good as their support staff and if the staff got lazy and uncaring, the work suffered. Charlie Higgins was loved by all of his staff and assistants, but he demanded excellence and if you were caught screwing around, Charlie would let you know it.

Charlie didn't want Himari to be walked over when it came to their staff and her future teams. He knew how good she was and how eventually she would leave and start her own group. Or maybe another high paying institution would steal her away and give her carte blanche when it came to equipment, staff and salary.

Himari was nervous, but she hid it as best she could, and she knew that Charlie had her back. This tagging would go by the numbers.

"*Polaris II* to *Rover*, Veitch what have you got for me?" Himari radioed.

"*Hey, Doctor Kohi, this is Yeates. Veitch has got the pole this time around. We're ready to go, got some fins in the water and waiting to see who's the hungriest, over.*"

"That's terrific, Tom. Let me know when you get a hit and we'll be ready for you. Keep your eye out for a white tip reef, that's the one we need to fill out our trifecta."

"*Roger, Yeates out.*"

Himari looked up at Charlie. He had been watching and listening. He gave her a thumbs up and mouthed, 'good job'. She mouthed back, 'thank you'.

"Rover to Polaris II, fish on," came over the radio.

"Kohi here *Rover*, what can we expect?"

"How does a beautiful meter and a half white tipper sound to you?"

"That's fantastic Tom. Well done. Bring it in," said Himari.

The male white tip reef shark was average size, about five feet long and approximately forty pounds. A non-aggressive species, the tagging of this one was a walk in the park. He was so eager to get off the cradle platform that he just about leapt off when the water hose was removed from his mouth. The crew was lucky. White tip reefs usually spent their days on the sea bottom, in caves, emerging at night to hunt eels, spiny lobsters, triggerfish, crabs, and bony fishes.

"Great job, crew!" yelled Charlie as he ran up to Himari. He took her in his arms and gave her a quick kiss. It shocked her a bit and she stepped back.

"Charlie, in front of the crew?"

"Yes, Himari, in front of the crew! I am so proud of you. Now let's get three more!"

"Okay everyone," Himari said as the blush faded from her cheeks. "You heard the boss, that's one down, three to go," she walked to the rail, holding up three fingers in the air.

Yeates and the *Rover* crew brought in two grey reef sharks for tagging. The crew made short work of them.

Doctor Bissette had come up on deck. After working for ten hours in the lab, she needed a breath of fresh air before turning in for a nap.

"Hi, Charlie," Bissette said as she walked up beside Doctor Higgins.

"Hi, Abby. Finally dragged yourself out of the lab, I see."

"I'm only onboard for a short time, so I wanted to get in as much lab time as possible. Samples from yesterdays four sharks are done and logged into the database."

"That's terrific. I wish you could stay with us for the entire tour. We could make you a full time member of the 'Shark Squad.'"

"'Shark Squad?' What's that?"

"It's an elite club that one has to earn one's membership in."

"And how do I do that?" she asked.

"Easy, my Canadian friend. You have to get your feet wet and tag a shark. We currently have seven members, with room for more. Of course numero uño is Mister Cooper, but we don't count him in our club," Charlie said gesturing towards Cooper.

"Mister Cooper has tagged a lot of sharks?"

"Cooper has over four hundred sharks under his belt. Shark tagging has been around since the nineteen forties, but Cooper has revolutionized it. The shark cradle platform is his idea and design."

"Wow, I wish I had more time to spend with him this trip."

"This has not been an everyday excursion. People have had a lot of things on their minds," Charlie said.

"Rover to Polaris II, fish on!"

"Kohi to Yeates, you're just going to make our day end sooner. We'll be ready," Himari said into her walkie-talkie.

"Himari, it's been way too easy. It's like the sharks want to be caught. We've got you something special this time, a great big hammer-head."

"'That's one of my favorites. Bring it onboard, over."

Himari looked up to the deck from the cradle platform. She saw Charlie talking to Abigail Bissette. Himari did not know her that well, but she didn't like how close Abby was standing next to Charlie.

"Himari, what did Rover get us this time?" Charlie asked.

"Yeates says it's a big, beautiful hammerhead!" she said to him.

"We've haven't tagged a hammer in awhile. I'll be right down if that's okay?"

"Sure, come on down and get your feet wet. You can show me your moves," Himari said.

Charlie Higgins excused himself from Doctor Bissette and headed down to the shark cradle. Along the way he passed by Cooper and XO Menard as they came out to the lower deck rail that was directly in front of the cradle. It was the second best seat in town.

"Hey fellas, we got ourselves a hammerhead."

"Then this will be a fun tag. Hey Charlie, watch out for the hammer, they can be very unpredictable, " Cooper reminded.

"I hear ya poppa," Charlie answered.

Charlie just about had time to get his water shoes on and step out on to the platform when the *Rover* pulled alongside with the cradle towing the shark fifty feet behind them.

"Charlie!" Veitch yelled from the *Rover*, "Keep an eye on this one. We've been dragging him hard the entire trip here. He was easy to catch, but now he's acting skittish."

"Thanks Rick, we'll keep an eye on him."

Charlie said to Himari, "It's all yours, run the board."

And run the checklist board she did. Himari had the cradle dropped and the shark brought onboard. While it was blinded and having water run over its gills, her team took blood and tissue samples, measurements, and gave it a routine physical exam.

Himari walked over to Charlie while the team was wrapping up the shark. "Charlie, why don't you release him?"

"You sure? This was your baby."

"I'm sure. I see that look in your eye. You've been dying to get your hands on a shark all day."

"And that, my dear, is why I love you so much."

Himari blushed again and then looked away and saw Abigail Bissette looking down at her and Charlie. This time nothing was going to bother her.

"Okay everyone, let's wrap up this shark, so that Doctor Higgins can send him on his way," Himari announced.

The team left the cradle platform removed the water hose from the shark's mouth.

"Bring the cradle down two feet, I'll guide him off," Higgins said.

Himari backed all the way to the base of the cradle, next to the ship's hull.

Charlie removed the towel from the shark's head. The hammerhead jerked in the air, but then quieted down as Charlie slowly walked him toward the submerged lip of the cradle.

"That's a good boy, you did really well. Go have some fun, we'll keep an eye on you from afar."

The hammerhead swam off into the sea as Charlie turned towards the crew and raised his arms in victory.

"That's a wrap for today, everyone. Drinks are on–"

Just then a fifteen-foot tiger shark leapt out of the water and onto the submerged port side of the cradle. It was moving at tremendous speed as it skipped through the two feet of water and slammed into Charlie Higgins. It bit and dragged him along the cradle. The only thing that saved him from going into the water was the far wall of the cradle. He hit it hard. Hard enough for him to bounce his head off of it, and bite through his tongue. Blood sprayed out of his mouth and splattered into the shark's eye.

"Charlie!" screamed Himari.

"No!" yelled Cooper.

The entire crew reacted in shock and disbelief.

Charlie began beating on the sharks sensitive nose and top of its head. It shook its head savagely, shredding more of Charlie's stomach and intestines. Charlie screamed as he aimed his next punch at the tiger's eye, and scored a direct hit. The shark shook free and scurried to the cradles edge, dropping into the water.

Cooper hopped over the rail onto the cradle platform and sloshed his way to the cradle's outer wall, "Charlie! Charlie!"

Charlie looked over to Matt. His hair was wet and plastered to his head. He was so pale, his face drained of color. Matt looked at Charlie's stomach and he could see shredded muscle and organs and there were loops of intestines on his lap. His head lolled on his shoulders as one leg dangled in the water. His right arm was thrown out from his side, his fingers just brushing the waters surface. For some reason, Charlie thought he could shove his intestines back into his torso, so he reached down and applied pressure. Blood was jetting out of his ruined abdomen, causing his blood pressure to drop, putting him into a state of pain-free euphoria.

"Charlie!" yelled Cooper. "I'm coming boy. I'm going to get you to safety."

Before Matt could move any closer, the tiger shark came out of the water, swallowing Charlie's right arm and biting into his shoulder. Charlie screamed out in pain, blood spraying from his mouth. The tiger pulled down and Charlie Higgins disappeared from the cradle, the water rippling with a mixture of foam and blood.

Menard started to climb over the rail, his damaged knees slowing him down, when he saw the fin coming in from the port side. Cooper was looking out to sea in the opposite direction.

"Cooper!" Menard yelled.

He lurched across the cradle deck as a seventeen-foot great white shark tried repeating to Cooper what the tiger did to Charlie. Fortunately the shark's larger mass slowed it down as it scraped along the wooden deck.

Menard tackled Cooper, sending both men ass-over-teakettle over the short outer wall as the great white snapped at the empty space where they had been standing.

The shark slid off the starboard side and disappeared into the water. Someone from the crew yelled for the cradle to be raised.

Cooper came up out of the water coughing and hacking up seawater. He wasn't quite sure what had happened, but now he realized he was in trouble. Cooper had gone all the way into the water while Menard had held onto the cradle's outer wall.

He started to turn towards the cradle when he saw the fin break the surface, aimed straight at him. He thought this is it, *the end!* But this was no ordinary fin. This one was discolored, pocked, and huge, standing four feet above the surface. This had to be the big radioactive shark. He had to see it. Cooper sank under the waves and hung in the water as the big shark swam towards him and then past. He looked into its dead, white eye. The same eye that Max had mentioned before. He could have sworn it was looking at him.

The shark was huge, forty feet at least, and its anatomy was oddly out of proportion. Its head and jaws were enormous, with messy snaggleteeth, a slim torso and rear body. It had a huge tail and overly long pectoral fins. One of those fins clipped Cooper and sent him tumbling in the water, knocking the breath out of his lungs, pushing him further down. Looking below he saw at least a hundred sharks swimming below the big shark, trailing like an entourage.

Cooper oriented himself and started to swim to the surface when he suddenly felt a vise grip on his arm. As he waited for the tearing of flesh and pain, he was instead lifted out of the water by Menard and dragged onto the outer wall of the cradle.

"I've got you, Matt, hang onto the wall." Menard turned and looked behind him to the crew, "Get this goddamn cradle out of the water!"

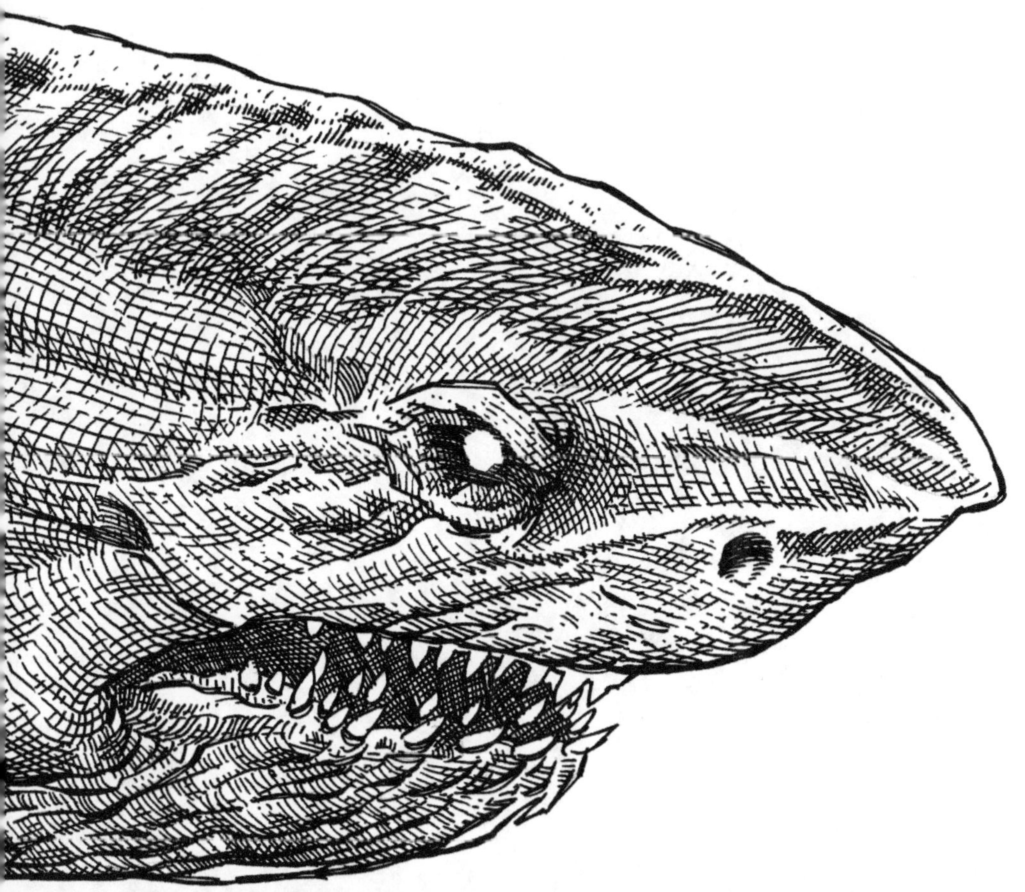

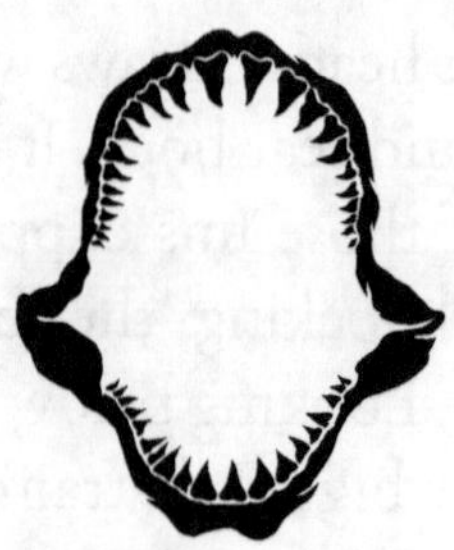

The snaggletooth swam along with his herd; sensing one prey had been carried away while another was floundering in the water. It was small and black; he was not sure if it was a seal or some other prey. He rose along the surface and it sink below, suspended in the current. It did not strike out, nor did it swim away. It looked at him, and he, at it. He smelled something different about this prey, so he pushed it away, and led his herd away from the large intruder, for now.

Chapter 22

The mood in the galley was dark and all conversations were kept low and hushed as Joey T. and his staff went around pouring coffee, tea and soft drinks. Johnson, Amenta and Markowski were at their usual table having been joined by navigator Kyle Richard and pilot Marty Malone.

"What can I pour ya, fellas?" Joey asked.

"The largest scotch you've got, Joey," Johnson said.

"Sorry guys no can do. Captain Dobbs ordered that no one gets served alcohol until he gives the all clear."

"Fuck that, man!"

"I know how you feel JJ, but Dobbs is my boss and he gets the last word."

"No problem, Joey," Malone added, "We understand how it is."

Kyle added, "We had ringside seats to the old man so we understand where's he's coming from."

"So he saw Higgins...?" Joey asked.

"Yeah," Kyle answered, "He was watching it from the bridge over the CCTV system. He was devastated. He hasn't lost a man in decades."

Paper added, "I was lucky to be below decks in the server room. I don't want to ever see anything like that."

Amenta looked at Richards and Malone and gestured, "The three of us were on the bridge and just about shit our pants when it happened."

"Count me as lucky as Paper. I was on the bow flying a drone and didn't see a goddamn thing. No sharks in the water at all," Johnson said.

"No sharks in sight... at all?" asked Kyle.

"None. I'd been looking all morning per Menard's orders," Johnson replied.

"Speaking of, he's got to have the biggest sack on the entire boat. He hopped that rail and saved Cooper's ass," Amenta said.

"Give it up for Cooper, too. Dude's 70 years old and was across the cradle in a couple seconds looking for Charlie," Malone trailed off.

At the mention of Charlie, the table got very quiet. Then Markowski asked, "Anyone know how Doctor Kohi is doing?"

Chapter 23

Himari Kohi sat on the edge of a sick bay bed, staring endlessly into space. Doctor Shane and her staff had changed her out of her wet clothes and dressed her in a hospital gown hoping to make her more comfortable.

"Hi Himari," Shane said as she came over to her patient. "Is there anything I can get you?"
Himari continued staring, not acknowledging the question.

"How about we get you to lay down and try to sleep? Sharon, can you help me?"

Nurse Sharon Young came over and helped spin Himari onto the bed and ease her back. Sharon drew up the blanket and made sure her head was settled on the pillow.

"Sharon, a word please?" Shane asked as she stepped away.
"Yes, Doctor."

Shane turned when she was far enough away for her patient not to overhear the conversation. "Sharon, keep an eye on her, make sure she gets anything she wants. I'm hoping some sleep will help her snap out of this trauma-induced fugue. I'm going down the hall to check on Cooper and Menard."

"Sure thing, Doctor Shane."

Shane went down a few doors to Exam room three. She drew back the curtain to find Cooper sitting on the edge of his bed, still dressed in his wet clothes, with Menard pacing the floor.

"What did I say, gentlemen? *Change out of your wet clothes, put on the gowns and lie down and relax.* Mister Cooper, you took a good smack to the head and Mister Menard, you're all scraped up, so will you both do as I asked?"

"Yes ma'am," replied Menard quietly as he sat on the room's other bed.

"Doctor Shane," Cooper said. "*I* respect your position and

medical knowledge, but *I* just had one of my guys killed by a shark. *I* was almost killed by one shark and *I* had a forty-foot radioactive shark give me the stink eye and bounce me off its fin. I've got to get up to the labs and check on my people, and then go after these sharks, not sit around here waiting for an aspirin and a lollipop!"

"Mister Cooper!" yelled Doctor Shane.

Menard rolled his eyes. He knew what was coming.

"*I* am going to treat you for your head contusion. *I* am going to treat Mister Menard for his lacerations. Then *I* am going to get you dry clothes and after that, *I* don't care where you go, do you understand me? *I* expect you to be back here in six hours because *I* am also going to put you under a concussion watch so that *I* can keep an eye on that thing you call a brain," Shane said as she poked Cooper's forehead.

Cooper sat in disbelief. He had spent the last forty-five years building up his reputation and starting up the Institute. He hadn't been spoken to like that since his mother. At a loss for words, tired and sore, he responded the only way he could at the time –

"Yes ma'am."

Doctor Shane glared at both men and then left the room, swishing the privacy curtain back in place.

Cooper looked over at Menard. "Thanks for saving me."

"You're welcome, asshole."

Cooper just silently nodded his head in agreement. "Yup."

Captain Dobbs was pacing the bridge of the *Polaris II* like a wild cat, his eyes darting between the forward windows and back to the CCTV monitors in front of his chair. He was looking for the sharks. Earlier, he had been pissed at them for the Gloria J. Now he was irate for them attacking his boat and crew. He was not a violent man, and he did not hold grudges, but these sharks had crossed the line. Now he wanted their heads.

"Amenta, any chatter from nearby ships?"

"No sir, all is quiet."

"Richards, what's our heading?"

"We're four miles off Brisbane at a heading due east, moving deeper into the Coral Sea."

"Amenta, shout out to your pal Johnson. I want him and his team of flyboys to have their drones up in the air around the clock. Have them go out a half mile from our location. Keep one or two in reserve, charging. I also want eyes on all four corners of this boat. Have Mister Coache recruit a few of the crew and put binoculars in their hands."

"Sonar!" snapped Dobbs.

"Yes sir," answered sonar operator Tom Wylie.

"Anything on screen?"

"No sir, nothing like what we're looking for."

"And what are we looking for?" sarcastically asked Dobbs, staring a hole through the sonar operator.

Wylie swallowed hard. He had only been on the *Polaris II* a couple of months and had never been put on the spot like this.

"A shark, sir."

"What kind of shark, Mister Wylie?"

"A huge radioactive shark sir, with at least a school of fifty sharks swimming with it."

"That is exactly what we are looking for, gentlemen." Dobbs said, addressing the entire Bridge crew. "And I want them bad. I want you to shout out if you see or hear anything. It doesn't matter how small or trivial you think it is. We are on high alert gentlemen. Let's get it done."

"Richards, I am going below decks to find our missing XO. You've got the Con, but if you spot anything –"

"We'll shout real loud and get you back up here, sir."

"Outstanding." Dobbs left the Bridge, taking most of the air with him.

"Holy shit," Wylie said quietly.

"Welcome to the *Polaris II*, kid," said Amenta.

Captain Dobbs found Cooper and Menard coming out of sick-bay, both had gotten into dry clothes. The scrapes on Menard's hands and arms had been cleaned and bandaged and Cooper was holding a cold pack to the right side of his head.

"There you are!" exclaimed Dobbs. "Are you okay?"

"We're fine, Rob, just a little banged up. I would have been in rougher shape if not for your XO," Cooper said.

"How about you, Steve. Everything A-Okay?" Dobbs asked.

"I'm fine, Captain. A little scraped up and I'll be icing my knees, but we're alive."

"No shit," Dobbs replied. "I saw it all on my monitors. What the fuck was that, an organized attack?"

"I think we need to have a sit down, Cap and compare notes," Cooper said. "I want to bring Johnson in on this. Kohi is still out of it so I want Doctor Bissette in on it, too. I'd also like to send your footage up to Pearl Island and have my niece, Bobbi take a look at it."

"Do you think that's smart? Don't we want to keep it only with our crew so we can control the situation?"

"Cap, I think Bobbi can give us some insight on this. My people in Pearl are professional There won't be any leaks."

"What do you think?" asked Dobbs, looking over to his XO.

"If Mister Cooper thinks his people can see something we didn't, then I say loop them in," Menard answered.

"Ok, Cooper," Dobbs said. "See Markowski down in the IT room. He can pull the footage for you and send it off to Pearl."

Chapter 24

To: bcooper@cisr.com
From: mcooper@cisr.com

Subject: Brisbane sharks

Hi Bobbi,

Things here have turned bad. We had a shark attack today and we lost Charlie Higgins. Everyone here is shocked and scared.

I'm sending you footage of the incident taken from our stern camera.

Prepare your self; it's not easy to watch. Bring in as few people as possible, keep this low profile. Get back to me as soon as you can. Any advice you have would be helpful.

Thanks,
Matt

Doctor Matthew Cooper
Cooper Institute for Shark Research
Miami, FL

Polaris II_stern_footage.mov

Chapter 25

Bubbles surround the diver, blinding him, as he tries to focus on the face of the man in front of him. It's a friendly, smiling face of a young man swimming towards him. Suddenly the face is one of horror as the bubbles continue to swirl and the diver feels the water around him surge. Then he feels the impact to his back as he is slammed forward. His arms and legs are flailing as something continues to drive him forward.

The diver looks at the surface and sees a dance of bubbles rising up it, looking to rejoin the gases above. The sunlight still manages to make it this far underwater, playing a kaleidoscope of colors all around.

He feels a pounding on his back, no, more like something biting him, but he doesn't feel any pain. The thing behind him is biting into his scuba gear as it continues to push him forward.

He is being savagely shaken side-to-side, his head is snapping left and right. He's confused, disoriented, what holds him? Then he's pushed forward even faster. He looks over his shoulder and sees grey skin and long pointed fins moving furiously in the water. Further away he sees a tail fin.

A shark!

It has bitten into his gear trying to get to him. The shark shakes him again. The diver thinks the shark is panicking. Its teeth are caught in the straps of his gear, and the metal air tank is in its mouth.

The diver is struggling to get himself free, reaching for anything that could help him. He finds the handle of his diver's knife and struggles to pull it from its scabbard. The shark rockets forward again, knocking his limbs back. The knife is free and in his fist. He can't swing around to strike, but he can reach over his shoulder.

He stabs randomly, hoping to hit his target. He feels the knife bite flesh and sees blood swirling in the water.

The diver knows he's in serious trouble. He can't free himself from his gear, not with the shark snarled in it. He needs the oxygen in the tank to survive yet it's protecting him from the shark's attack.

He is surrounded by more and more bubbles. He starts to panic and over-exhale into his regulator. If he keeps this up he'll black out and nitrogen bubbles will spread into his tissues, causing muscle pain and possible death.

He turns the blade around in his grip and starts thrusting downward and back, hoping to hit the shark behind its jawbone or to maybe hit an eye. He feels the flesh give and the shark reacts by shaking him even more.

How can this horribly tasting Thing in its mouth bring on so much pain? Why can't it let go of it? The bitter, smooth metal rubs along its tongue, the taste unlike anything it's ever had in its mouth. Swirling black tendrils continue to hit its nose, sensitive eyes and electroreceptors. Sharp pain travels all along its head.

Stinging pain, stabbing in its head – what is the Thing hitting it with? It must shake the Thing some more, must get loose of this tangle.

Sharp pain under its lower jaw. The Thing is hitting it there. Painful strikes along its jawbone! Must shake, shake to be free. Do not care about eating this Thing anymore.

Must! Be! Free!

The diver thinks the blade-strikes to the shark's jaw are working. It's still trying to shake free, but it's slowing down.

The straps to his scuba gear have torn loose and the shark has jolted clean away. Finally, he's free!

The big fish swims off leaving the diver to compose himself. He looks around to get his bearings. He is near an old wrecked fishing boat. He can't make out the name too well, the salt water has eaten away most of it. He can read the last two letters, 'C', and 'A'. The letter before the 'C' might be an 'R' or a 'P', but he can't tell. All he can do is lean against the wreck and try to control his breathing, while keeping an eye out for the shark.

He hopes that it's grown frustrated and has swam away after some other prey. He looks out to the murky water and sees a figure. It's the shape of a man coming his way; it's a diver! Is it the young man he saw before the attack? His head is pounding; he knows he has nitrogen bubbles building up in his system. He shakes his head to clear it and sees the other diver coming closer.

Suddenly, from the corner of his eye, he sees the shape of the shark, swimming towards the other diver. What can he do? Both the shark and the diver are too far away for him to reach in time.

What to do, what to do?

The diver starts to bang on the hull of the wrecked ship. He is frantically pounding, trying to get the shark's attention. He sees that the other diver has seen the shark and is now lying on the ocean bottom, trying to get out of reach.

Pound, kick, and try to create as much noise as possible.

The shark jerks to the right, towards the sound of banging. It has worked it's coming his way. The other diver is safe for now.

The shark comes directly at the diver, building up speed. It's still in pain from the numerous wounds along its head and jaw, and all it wants is to make the pain stop.

The diver has no way of escaping this, but at least he knows that the other diver is safe...

...Richie is safe and Matt can die knowing his brother would go on to greatness.

The shark slams Cooper in the chest, plowing him back into the deserted wreck. The waterlogged timbers of the hull implode, crumbling and stirring up a cloud of debris.

Cooper knows his ribs are shattered, and one lung is punctured. He can't move his legs, and his back is probably broken.

The shark is biting, eating, trying to make the pain stop...

Cooper bolts up from his nightmare, the same nightmare that haunted him throughout his late twenties and thirties. He thought he would never have it again, but his near death yesterday brought it back, and this time, Richie survived. This time the shark found its prize and tore him apart.

He sits in his bed sweating, hyperventilating, and crying. The past fifty-five years and the events of yesterday, all catch up with him at once.

Chapter 26

XX: *Are you there? Things have gone to shit here.*

CooperIndustries: Hello my friend. What's going on?

XX: *Charlie Higgins is dead!*

CooperIndustries: What happened?

XX: *He got eaten by a fucking shark!*

CooperIndustries: Language, my dear.

XX: *Give me a break. Charlie was slammed by a tiger shark, had his guts chewed on, then the fucker came back and dragged him under.*

CooperIndustries: Anyone else get hurt?

XX: *Matt Cooper went overboard trying to save him. The monster shark took a swipe at him. Menard saved his ass.*

CooperIndustries: Matt almost got eaten by one of his prize sharks. That's almost too bad. Menard you say?

XX: *Yeah, the XO. He dragged him off the shark cradle.*

CooperIndustries: I'll have to look into your XO Menard, see what makes him tick. Look into how I can hurt him.

XX: *You've got to be kidding!*

CooperIndustries: Tell me about this monster shark.

XX: *It's freaking big. Bigger than a great white. We rescued some guys off of a boat. The big shark and a bunch of other sharks attacked their fishing boat. Wiped out most of the crew. Tooth sample came back as radioactive.*

CooperIndustries: Radioactive? That's interesting. There haven't been any nuclear incidents near Australia in decades.

XX: *Everyone is wigged out.*

CooperIndustries: Keep it under control. Can you send me a report??

XX: *Give me a few hours. The science lab is all a mess and people aren't thinking straight. I'll send what I can when it's safe.*

CooperIndustries: Send it to me. I'll make sure it ends up in the right hands.

XX: *Shit is getting real here.*
There's a shitload of sharks out there!

CooperIndustries: Don't worry. I know Matthew, he won't let anyone else get hurt.

XX: *You can say that being a thousand miles away, but you're not here on the friggin' boat.*

CooperIndustries: Just try and relax. Do your best with the info packet. I'll make sure a generous gift is deposited into your account.

XX: *Okay…I appreciate that. Once I can get my hands on the files, I'll get them to you.*

CooperIndustries: Thank you my boy. Your hard work and your loyalty will be rewarded. We will be speaking soon.

Chapter 27

The stern conference room of the *Polaris II*.

Cooper had called together senior staff as well as crewmembers that had been directly involved with the search for the sharks.

Seated around the conference table were Cooper, Dobbs, Menard, Shane, Johnson, Amenta, Bissette, and Markowski. Cooper started the meeting. "Ladies and gentlemen, we have had some dark times this trip and we need to work hard to make things right.

We will all miss Doctor Charlie Higgins. His death was tragic, and his expertise and his passion will be missed. We are still searching for the sharks and we have confidence that we will find them–"

"And then we kill the shit out of them, right?" Johnson added.

"We need to discuss that amongst senior–"

"No! Fuck that! Those shits killed Charlie and 'King Shark' tried to kill you. Aren't you pissed? Don't you want to find them and kill them all?"

"That will be enough, Mister Johnson!" ordered Captain Dobbs.

"It's alright, Captain," said Cooper. "We all feel the way Jon feels and I appreciate him voicing it."

"Doctor Shane, how is Doctor Kohi doing," asked Cooper?

"Himari has suffered severe trauma and her mind has shut down. She does not respond verbally and has not moved on her own since the incident. We're keeping her comfortable and we've set her up with an I.V. to keep her fluids and electrolytes balanced. I feel it's a waiting game until her mind thinks she's ready to deal with it."

Cooper said, "Thank you Doctor.

Mister Menard, where do we stand with the ship?"

"The ship is running perfectly. The shark cradle got a little banged up, but it's operational–"

"No one is going to use the cradle or go in the water and that is final!" Dobbs ordered.

The room became silent for a few seconds. Captain Dobbs knew that his words had been heard.

"Mister Menard?" Cooper asked.

"The crew is spooked but they're doing their jobs. I've spoken to the science department heads and they're keeping their people busy collating the new data. You've got some good people there, Cooper."

Cooper nodded his head in agreement. "Paper, how are the satellite and radiological searches going?" Cooper asked.

"The satellites are currently out of range but we should have two back in the area within a couple hours and then we can continue scanning. We took our eye off the ball during the tagging and didn't see the sharks coming."

"We'd been busting our balls for days searching and waiting, so no one is to blame," Amenta added. "Wylie had been going non-stop on sonar and nothing pinged. We think the sharks had been swimming deep and under our wake, using the ship as a blind spot."

"Hey man that's fucking impossible, they're just animals. You're giving them too much credit," said Johnson.

"Doctor Bissette, Mister Cooper, you are our shark experts at this meeting, what do you think?" asked Dobbs.

Doctor Bissette thought for a couple of seconds and then said, "Sharks are very smart and no one gives them credit for that. People think they're evil eating machines, and they're not. Are they smart enough to swim under the ship to avoid our systems? Maybe. But maybe we're reading too much into their behavior. Maybe it's just coincidence."

"I would agree with Doctor Bissette any other time, but this is different," said Cooper. "We all feel it, and except for Johnson, we've all kept it to ourselves."

Johnson sat back and smiled like the Cheshire cat while Markowski looked at him, shaking his head in amusement.

"I think we need to double down on our search for this herd of sharks. We need to look behind, in front of, and below the *Polaris II.*

If what Amenta says is correct, then we need to adjust our satellite and sonar readings," Cooper stated.

"I also think we need to continue the drone searches, sending them out to their limits," Menard added. "Johnson, what's the status on your drones?"

"I've got two fully juiced. One is on the charger now and the fourth had a collision with a seagull, so I have some rotor damage to repair. I can get 20-25 minutes from each depending on the weather. Heavy winds slow them down and drain the batteries. I can have them all up and running first thing in the morning."

Menard asked, "Based on Amenta's comments, can you rig up some cameras that we can mount underwater at the bow and stern? I want to be able to keep an eye out for the sharks in their element."

"Sure, I can set them up with magnetic mounts below the water line–"

"And I can run lines from them to the server room and tap into our CCTV system and send the feed to the Bridge," added Markowski.

"That's great, fellas. So that's where we stand for now. Captain Dobbs, anything from you?" Cooper asked.

"I want to make things very clear to everyone at this table, especially to you Mister Cooper. This is no longer a research excursion: this has become a search and destroy mission. Do I make myself clear?"

"Captain, I think if we remove 'King Shark' out of the picture the other sharks will go back to their normal routines. So yes, perfectly clear," answered Cooper.

"All right everyone, you know what you've got to do, so let's get on with it. Find those sharks," ordered Dobbs.

Everyone got up to leave the conference room. Markowski sidled next to Johnson with Amenta close behind, 'King Shark', you had to name it, didn't you?" Paper said.

Johnson threw up his arms in despair, "Someone had to, I'm the most creative here."

Amenta added, "Your creativity is going to have 'King Shark' eating your ass."

Chapter 28

To: mcooper@cisr.com
From: bcooper@cisr.com

Subject: Brisbane sharks

Uncle Matt, are you insane? What did you think you were doing jumping into the water?

I am so sorry to hear about Charlie, he was such a nice guy. When he visited us at Pearl last year, he had all of the women here falling in love with him. My best to his family.

So we watched the video. It was truly horrible, but what we saw was unusual shark behavior. Sharks are generally shy and will back away from machines and man-made items. Those two sharks didn't care where they were; they just wanted to get to someone.

We were all floored by that large shark. We only saw it's dorsal and caudal fins, but seeing them proved to us here, that the shark is sick. Its skin is mottled and diseased and there are pieces of the fins missing, but not from bites.

I wish I could have seen it close up to look for other symptoms of radiation sickness. Send us anything your team comes up with and we'll go through it and give you our impressions.

Please take care of yourself, no more heroics! I want to see you when you get back.

Bobbi
Doctor Roberta Cooper
Cooper Institute for Shark Research
Pearl Island, MA

Chapter 29

Cooper was tired and sore, and all he wanted to do was lay down and sleep, but he checked his e-mail and saw the message from his niece Bobbi. She truly cared for him. It was a nice feeling. Cooper had never married or had any children; he always felt that the sharks were his children and he needed to know everything about them, so his personal life took a backseat.

Bobbi was his brother Alan's daughter and the only one in that family that he stayed in touch with. He had not spoken to Alan or his wife Madison in ten years, and even longer since he had spoken to Bobbi's sister and brother.

Bobbi was the only one in the family who understood his passion for the sea and marine biology, and even though her focus was more on studying the death of animals, she could keep up with any other area of marine biology.

Cooper was almost ready to shut his laptop down when he began to think of Pearl, and Ellen Brady. She was a good person and had always treated him like family; it had been too long since he last saw her. Ellen's was a tragic life; uprooted from her home in Pennsylvania, transplanted to a lonely, isolated island off the coast of Massachusetts, and left with no friends. In time she became part of the community, and her husband and two boys filled her time. Eventually she found that she enjoyed real estate and development and her career started to take off.

It was the sudden death of her husband Marvin, to a heart attack that shook her world. Later, the violent death of her son Dean sent her running from Pearl to stay with her son Michael in Bermuda. Tragedy and heartbreak followed her there but she was able to rise up above it and returned to Pearl where she restarted her real estate career and lived a quiet life.

Cooper needed to reach out to her, to just say hello and remember when life was a little simpler. The nightmare from the previous night forced him to.

To: ebrady@bradydevelopment.com
From: mcooper@cisr.com

Subject: Hello from Australia

Hi Ellen,

How are you doing? I hear from my niece Bobbi that the weather there is cold and rainy. Things here in Australia are sunny and warm; it's spring here below the equator. I am on the *Polaris II* off the coast of Brisbane and we're working hard down here.

Damn if some of these kids are spoiled.

I was thinking of you and your family and I wanted to say hi and see how you were.

I hope your business is doing well, try and retain some of Pearl's charm.

Did it ever have charm?

Take care,
Matt
Doctor Matthew Cooper
CEO/Cooper Institute for Shark Research
Miami, FL

He did it.

She probably won't write back to him, but at least he reached out. As Cooper drifted off to sleep a faint memory surfaced and bobbed along in his dreams, something to do with snails, and Michael Brady and Bermuda.

Chapter 30

Pamela Delaney was working late, going over the expenses for the Institute. She was also looking into Matthew's patents and making sure that the monthly and quarterly payments were being made. She had some great manufacturers licensing the patents, but no matter how good they were, no one was completely trusted.

The patents were also not just being licensed in the USA. There were contracts with at least three manufacturers in China, five in Australia, two in New Zealand and at least ten throughout Europe. This involved different time zones, geographic challenges, different spoken and written languages, and challenging personalities. Some were big money contracts to larger companies, while over the years; Matthew allowed smaller companies, more Mom and Pops than bigger LLC's, to use his patents. He always favored the underdogs, but he also knew to keep the Institute running, he needed the bigger contracts.

Pamela was so focused on the computer screen in front of her she hardly heard her phone ringing. She ignored it like she often did, because she knew her assistant, Stephanie, would be guarding the gate and would not allow any trivial calls through. Then she realized her desk phone was not ringing, the sound was coming from her purse, and that it was after hours so Steph had gone home for the night. She reached down and picked up her Gucci Sylvie crocodile top hand bag and took out her 'burner' phone. She was advised to pick up the cheap, almost traceless phone, for when she and her benefactor needed to talk.

"Hello my dear."
That voice. No matter how many times she heard it, she could hear

the entitlement rolling through it.

"Hi. It's good to hear from you. I needed the distraction from all of this paperwork," she said, gesturing at the piles of files on her desk and at her computer screen.

"I won't take up too much of your time, I know you're busy on both fronts. I just wanted to let you know you'll be receiving a packet of reports from the Polaris II."

"Your spy must be working overtime with the speed that I've been getting these reports."

"Yes, the information has been moving fast and furious from Australia. This latest batch will certainly help take our plan one giant step further."

Damn, he avoided my question of the identity of his spy.

"I look forward in reading the reports. I need something solid so we can move forward."

"My dear, when you read these, it will make our case as solid as the Walls of Constantinople.

Chapter 31

"Good morning sunshine," Jon Johnson said as he came up behind Paper in the crew hallway.

"And good morning to you too, twinkle toes. How much did we drink last night?" Paper Markowski answered as they stumbled along the starboard rail of the ship.

"Shit, too much bourbon and whiskey. Good thing we used our private stock and didn't have to rely on Joey T. to get us the good stuff. At least we got our groove on for one night. Come on, help me with these underwater cameras."

The mounting and installation of the underwater cameras went perfectly. One on the bow, three feet below the water line and one on the stern, mounted at a similar depth. The mounting was a little tricky. The natural earth magnets held well, but Johnson had to use an extendable gaff and hook to put them in place. He hung over the rail keeping one eye on the hook and one on the water, scanning for fins.

Markowski then took the heavy gauge USB cables from the cameras and ran them along the outer structure of the ship. He then added extension cables with modified couplings and brought them inside. He'd go back and use heat shrink to waterproof the couplings.

Connecting the cameras to his server rack was easy and sending their feed to the Bridge was done in ten minutes.

Johnson and Markowski stood back and looked at their handy work.

"Nice job, big guy, that looks great. Dobbs will have some great views fore and aft," Johnson said.

"Until your magnets let go and we lose the cameras to the bottom of the sea," Paper said, smirking.

"Or a freaking shark sneaks up and eats them. Come to the stern with me, I gotta relieve one of my drone guys."

Chapter 32

To: mcooper@cisr.com
From: ebrady@bradydevelopment.com

Subject: re: Hello from Australia

Hello Matt,

We're good here. The business is going well, we've broken ground on two new developments this past month. I ran into Bobbi a couple weeks ago at the market. She and some of your people were shopping for the Institute. It was good to see her; she's a delightful young woman.

I was surprised to hear from you. I've been thinking of you and the last time we saw each other here on the island.

My life is good, Matt. I try to take it day by day and keep my head held high. Please don't take what I am about to say to heart, but we need to stop talking. I have my life under control and when I hear from you or anyone else from my past, I sink into a crippling depression. It's not you, it's me and I have to take care of myself.

Please take care of yourself. Your last message sounded forced like you were trying to protect me from something.

I will always fondly remember your friendship.
Ellen,

BTW, Pearl Island never had any charm.

Chapter 33

The Mako was swimming in small circles while it waited for its moment. It glanced down and saw its giant leader below, slowly rising. He could not believe how big and powerful the snaggletooth was, or why he felt he should follow it. His pulse quickened when he saw his leader, but he also felt his hunger decrease and his desire to mate completely disappear.

The two sharks waited below the large floating object, their tail fins twitching back and forth. They were moving slowly so oxygenated water would still pass over their gills. The current brought the scents of one hundred and twenty other sharks to them. All of these sharks were following one leader, and waiting for their chance to show the giant how loyal they were.

There was a splash from above; a small alien object had landed in the water. The giant swam up along the Mako and gently bumped it with his pectoral fin. There were smaller splashes above them and the object was moving towards the larger object. They waited a few more seconds and then...the time was now...GO!

Johnson and Markowski had made it to the stern of the boat, near the shark cradle. Drone specialist Michael Rivera was piloting one of the drones back but was struggling against a crosswind.

"Hey Jon, this little bitch is giving me a hard time," Rivera said.

"I can see that. How's the charge on the battery?"

"Lower than expected. I think there might be a problem with the battery. Either it's shot and not holding a charge, or some salt water got in and has corroded the contacts."

"Let me see the controller."

Rivera handed the controller to Johnson, who did his best to get the drone onboard. It was swaying in the wind and losing propulsion. Then the power cutout and the drone crashed in the water, eight feet shy of the cradle.

"Damnshitfuckdamn!"

"You almost stuck the landing," Markowski noted.

"Yeah, har-dee-har-har. It lost all of its juice and now we're down a drone," Johnson said.

"We could fish it out. There's a gaff over here and it would save us all the paperwork and thousands of dollars," suggested Rivera.

Johnson looked over at the gaff, looked at the drone floating in the ocean, and started to weigh the odds of retrieving it.

"You know if Dobbs catches us anywhere near the cradle or the water, he's going to skin our asses," Johnson said, looking at the other men.

"I'm not going to tell him, how about you Mike?" Paper said.

"Nope, not me."

Johnson said, "All right, let's get that gaff and retrieve that drone."

Jon, Mike, and Paper headed down to the cradle with the gaff. The drone was now floating seven feet from the open side of the cradle, off the starboard side. One of the rotors had been bent in the crash.

"That doesn't look too bad," said Paper.

"Yeah, it could have been worse except once I get it back and on my bench, I've got to dry it out. If that doesn't work, then I gotta swap out all of the electronics. Shit, that's going to take hours," Jon noted.

Johnson reached out with the gaff, out over the water, "Well, here goes," he said. "One of you guys grab my belt and hang on so I don't go for a swim."

"I've got you. Mike, be ready to grab that drone when he get's it close," Paper said.

Johnson poked and prodded the drone with the hooked gaff.

He was reaching out farther than he wanted to but he needed to get that drone back.

"Come on, baby, almost there."

Johnson had hooked one of the propellers and was slowly dragging it, taking care not to let the hook slip. He was leaning way past the edge of the cradle, balancing on his left foot while Paper was hanging onto his right ankle.

"Let me hang out just a little bit more, I want to make sure I–"

Johnson glanced downward at his reflection on the water's surface, when his focus changed and he was suddenly looking at a mako shark rocketing up towards him, its jaws wide open.

"Oh shit," he said softly.

The shark exploded out of the water, grabbing Johnson's head and upper torso with its jaws. The strike was so powerful that he was ripped in half, his upper torso carried away in the shark's mouth.

Markowski freaked-out and let go of Johnson's leg. His lower half hung in mid air, his legs not knowing what had happened.

The shark hit its apex at twelve feet and then fell back in the water, the same time Jon Johnson's lower torso and legs fell to the cradle deck. His intestines and other internal organs that had not been ripped a part, started to slowly fall into the ocean.

Suddenly his intestines went taught and were pulled into the water; the rest of Johnson's body followed.

There was a feeding frenzy at the cradle's edge and Rivera and Markowski jumped back.

"Jon!"

"No, motherfuckers!"

"Jon, no, no, no!"

Mike and Paper edged away from the water and climbed the ladder to the rear deck. They both were in shock. Johnson was a good man, a good friend.

Both men started to head inside to find Menard, Cooper or Dobbs when Paper looked back to where his friend was killed. No sharks were visible, just the gaff and drone floating in the water.

Chapter 34

"What the fuck happened?" yelled Dobbs. He was on the bridge with Menard, Cooper, Rivera and Markowski. The rest of the bridge crew had been dismissed. Amenta went begrudgingly; he and Johnson had joined the crew at the same time and had bonded right away.

"I want to know what happened? What part of 'No one goes near the water' did either of you not understand?"

"Captain Dobbs, we just wanted to get the drone back onboard. We didn't see any sharks and…".

"And *now* another member of my crew is dead, Markowski!"

"Sir, we know we were ordered away from the water, but we thought it was safe–" Rivera added.

"Well Rivera, I guess it wasn't safe was it? Of all the stupid, irresponsible, half-ass stunts…"

"Look Captain," Markowski stepped forward towards Dobbs. He had eight inches over the Captain and close to one hundred pounds on the man and was clearly all fired up.

"You lost a crew member and we lost a friend. We were there; we saw it happen. How do you think we feel about this? I'll never forget what I saw. So whatever punishment you've got in mind will pale next to what happened on that deck."

Markowski stared down at the Captain, fire in his eyes. Menard stepped up behind him, ready to restrain him any way he could, while Cooper stepped between Markowski and Dobbs.

"Markowski," Cooper said. No reaction.

"Paper." That got his attention. His eyes shifted away from Dobbs, over to Cooper. His face relaxed and his hunched, tense shoulders dropped. Menard stepped back but stayed at the ready.

Cooper reached up and put a hand on Paper's big shoulder.

"Why don't you head to your room and lay down for a while. I'll make sure Doctor Shane stops by to check on you," Cooper said.

Markowski took a minute to take it all in. He nodded to Cooper and Captain Dobbs, then left the bridge, his head hanging on his chest.

"Rivera," Menard said. "Why don't you go with him and grab some rack time for yourself. We'll talk later."

"Yes, sir."

That left Cooper, Menard and Dobbs on the bridge alone.

"We have to head back to Brisbane," Dobbs said.

"Captain, we've still got a lot of research to follow up on and the sharks are still out there," Cooper pleaded.

"Cooper, I've got two dead men, one of mine and one of yours. Shit, I don't even have any bodies to bury because the fucking sharks ate them! I have to keep the well being and safety of the crew in mind and the best place to do that will be ashore in Brisbane."

Captain Dobbs turned to his XO. "Mister Menard, get the rest of the bridge crew back up here except for Amenta. I want him away from all of this and I want him checked on. Get a course plotted for Brisbane, I want to get the hell out of here."

"Yes sir," Menard said and left the bridge.

"Matt, we have to get these people to safety. Once we do that, we can have the Coast Guard or the Aussie Navy come out and blow the fuck out of these sharks. Afterwards, you can have any chunks you want to dissect and test, but for now, my orders are to head in."

"Alright, Bob. I'll get my people squared away and let them know."

Cooper left the bridge knowing that this was not going to end here. Even he could not foretell the disaster that was on the horizon.

Chapter 35

The *Polaris II* had made a slow 180-degree turn and was heading back to Brisbane; navigation had plotted a course out of the Coral Sea, and estimated a 4-day trip back to port.

Menard had the crew on emergency status, and all personnel had been ordered away from the shark cradle. Watches had been set up along the rail with binoculars and drones.

The *Polaris II* had a small armory; four men were stationed along the deck armed with 45 automatics and AR-15s. Captain Dobbs was not going to let anyone else get hurt on his ship; his orders were shoot to kill any sharks that were spotted.

Cooper had checked in with his research team. Everyone was going through the latest shark tagging information. Markowski had returned from some downtime, and he and Amenta had joined the science team as they tracked the tagged sharks using the satellites. All eight of the tagged sharks had stopped moving and their vital signs had stopped.

"Anyone want to take a guess on why we're not getting any data on these tagged sharks?" Markowski asked.

Doctor Samuel Grier was the first to offer his opinion, "The batteries on the tags are good for up to 5 years, so it's not a tech problem. I have an idea, but no one is going to like it."

"I hate to hear words like that," Amenta chimed in.

"Sam, please tell us your idea," Cooper said.

The short, bespectacled scientist said, "The only thing I can think of is, the other sharks killed them and left them behind so we couldn't track them."

After he said those words, everyone in the lab got quiet for a few seconds.

"That's silly, that's giving the sharks too much credit. Shit! I'm starting to sound like Johnson," Paper said.

"I think Sam is right," Cooper said. "It's a smart move but I don't think it's to keep us from tracking them."

"Then why do it?" Sam asked.

"Eight sharks were handled by us and had tags attached to their dorsal fins. Maybe it was the other sharks targeting them because they had something alien attached to their bodies.
Maybe they smelled different and that meant they were a threat, so they had to be removed."

"It sounds better when you say it," Sam said, "but I still think those eight sharks were targeted.

"I guess we'll never know," Cooper added.

Matt Cooper was on the bridge standing beside Dobbs. The bridge crew was on high alert manning sonar and radar, as well as the communications station. Ed St. Onge had been brought up from engineering to take over the radio station, leaving Amenta down in the science labs. All outside watches had reported no shark sightings. Crewman Lyla Jenkins had been stationed watching the underwater cameras that Johnson had rigged up; both monitors were clear.

"How we doing, Captain?" asked Cooper.

"We're looking good, Mister Cooper; no sightings, the ship is running well and the crew is performing perfectly. How goes things below with your people?"

"As good as possible. They're keeping busy going over the results of our tagging. Markowski and Amenta are still searching the satellite feed for any of the sharks and the Institute is waiting for any new information."

"Have all of your reports been secure to the Institute?" Dobbs asked.

"They have. Markowski set up quite the encryption system and firewall so no one besides our people have a clue of what's going on out here."

"Excellent news, we can't afford to—"

"Captain Dobbs?"

"What is it, Jenkins?"

Lyla Jenkins was monitoring the underwater camera system, stationed to Dobbs' left. She was in her mid-twenties, with short, strawberry blonde hair and bright, blue eyes. She had shown a desire to learn as much as she could, and often thought outside the box. She also had a background in telecommunications making her the right person to keep the camera system running while Markowski was busy.

"Captain, I've got movement nine meters behind us, approximately three meters below the surface."

"We're getting it here on sonar, too," Wylie reported.

"What do you see, Jenkins?" Dobbs turned and asked.

"Blurry shapes, moving back and forth, looks to be at least a dozen. None of them are getting close enough for a good look, sir."

"Sonar?"

"Nothing certain here either, sir. It's like they know our range and are staying just out of our sights," Wylie responded.

"Don't give me that shit, mister! These are fucking sharks, not PhDs. Get me a straight sonar reading so we can track them down and kill them!"

The bridge became deathly silent as Captain Dobbs' irrate order flowed over them. Even Cooper and Menard were left momentarily speechless.

"Alright, people," Menard broke in. "Let's get on the sonar, keep an eye on the cameras, and let's get some answers. Radio, keep an ear open for chatter from any nearby ships and navigation, let's get this big beauty back to port."

Captain Dobbs looked at his crew and then to his XO. Menard was covering his ass and was making sure the crew stayed focused. Cooper was looking at him with an inquisitive look, but Dobbs ignored him and looked out towards the sea. All he wanted right now was to get this ship and its crew home.

Chapter 36

To: mcooper@cisr.com
From: bcooper@cisr.com

Subject: re: Brisbane sharks

Hi Uncle Matt,

I've been going over all of the research your people onboard *Polaris II* has been sending me. It sounds like you've run into something no one has ever seen before. It's like there is communication between your 'King Shark' and the herd of sharks swimming with him. This is mind-blowing and unprecedented. This kind of research will keep the Institute going for years, hell, maybe decades.
I have to be honest with you; I'm scared for you and your crew. I think this is a dangerous situation and I think you need to get the hell out of that area. I hope your Captain is taking precautions to keep the crew safe. It got me thinking about what you can do to protect yourselves.
Michael Brady had an incident in Bermuda while he was doing research on the migration of snails. He ran into a shark and to protect himself, he rigged a beacon that sent electrical impulses through the shark's body, driving it crazy. What if you tried this in Brisbane? It's a long shot but maybe it will save your ass.

Take care and reach out to Michael.
Snailsking462@gmail.com

Luv,
Bobbi
Doctor Roberta Cooper
Cooper Institute for Shark Research
Pearl Island, MA

Chapter 37

Cooper was in the galley getting some coffee when his phone pinged Bobbi's e-mail. She seemed very concerned about him, and that made him love her even more. He had heard about Michael Brady's incident with a shark but he didn't know about a beacon. He had considered trying to dart 'King Shark" and kill it with strychnine nitrate, but he was unsure of the dosage. Now that the situation had worsened, he was unsure that they could get close enough to the shark's mouth or gills to inject the poison.

He hadn't spoken to Michael in many years. He had never been close to the Brady boys; but maybe it was time. Desperation can sometimes make us do things we don't want to do.

It wouldn't hurt to have a Plan A and a Plan B. First he would speak with Doctor Bissette about the dosage she thought would work on the large shark. Then he would speak to Menard about who his best marksman was. Maybe, just maybe, he wouldn't need Michael Brady's contraption.

Lyla Jenkins was monitoring the underwater cameras when she saw more defined shapes; sharks were following the ship.

She looked over to Wylie, "Tom, what do you see?"

Wylie had been at the sonar station for 14 hours and was exhausted, but the new hits on his screen got his adrenaline pumping.

"Multiple readings; they just came out of nowhere. I've got at least a dozen or more at the stern and just as many on our flanks. No big ping so I think 'King Shark' is laying low."

"Keep an eye on your screens, Wylie and Jenkins. Anything on the forward camera?" Dobbs asked.

"Nothing there, sir, looks like they are all behind us," Lyla said.

"St. Onge, contact XO Menard, and have him reposition his armed men to the stern. At the first sign of sharks breaking the surface, have them open fire."

"Aye, sir," answered the radioman.

"Malone, see if you can get us a little more speed out of the engines."

"Yes, Captain."

Jenkins was monitoring both the fore and aft cameras when a mako shark surged forward and took out the rear camera. Last thing on the screen was an open mouth and lots of teeth before going black.

"Oh dammit!"

"What's wrong, Jenkins?" asked Dobbs.

"A shark just ate our rear facing camera and–"

The forward facing camera went black as another shark took it out.

"Shit, they just took out our forward camera too, sir."

"Okay, I've had enough of this shit–" said Captain Dobbs when he was interrupted by a loud thump felt even up on the bridge.

"What the hell was that?" he said.

Another thump followed by a dozen more thumps.

Dobbs turned to Malone, "pilot, slow to one third,"

"Yes sir."

Something was banging on the hull of the ship. Dobbs knew it was not mechanical. It was clearly something in the water and he had a feeling he knew what it was.

"Radio, any report from Menard?"

"No, sir," answered Stonge. "I paged him and tried ringing the phones in the rear quarters but no one is picking up."

"Alright then, I'll head back to the stern and see what's going on."

He turned towards the navigator and said, "Richards, you've got the con until either Menard or myself return. Keep us on course to Brisbane as best you can."

"Aye, sir."

Captain Dobbs left the bridge from the side door and proceeded along the outside deck, listening to the thumps as they grew in intensity along the ship's hull. He stopped and looked over the rail below to the water's surface. He thought he saw fins and a lot of swimming shapes.

Suddenly Coache ran up to him from the rear of the ship.

"Captain, it's the freaking sharks, they're ramming into the hull!"

"What? Where abouts, Mister Coache?"

"Towards the stern, sir. We saw some fins and then they started to ram us. They mean business, they're hurting themselves; there's blood in the water."

All of a suddenly the ship lurched rapidly a few times and then lost forward momentum.

"What the hell?" Dobbs shouted.

Both men stumbled on their feet, grasping the rail so not to fall down.

"Come with me Coache, we're heading back to the bridge."

Captain Dobbs and the crewman made their way along the deck to the side door and entered the bridge.

"Report!"

Malone said, "We've lost forward propulsion, sir. I don't know what's going on, the engines are still spinning, but we're losing speed."

"Any report from Mister—"

XO Menard entered the bridge from the rear door, having come up from the stern and through the ship.

"Captain, we've got a major problem. The sharks have fouled the propellers. It looks like a group of them committed hari-kari and threw themselves into the blades, damaging them. Without being able to dive down there and see the problem, I'm guessing the propeller blades are broken and the shafts are bent. Without them, we're going to be adrift shortly."

"You've got to be kidding me."

"No sir. We saw blood and bits in the water."

"Captain, excuse me?" asked Jenkins.

"What is it?"

"We have a couple more underwater cameras in supply. We

could rig them on gaffs and use them to see the damage. Guaranteed the sharks will try and eat them, but if all we need is a quick look, it might work."

Captain Dobbs stood for a few seconds weighing the idea and made his decision.

"Jenkins, I want you to get with Markowski and rig the cameras. Mister Menard, I want your best able-bodied man on the gaff with a safety line on him. Have every armed crew member at the ready to take out any shark they see."

"Captain, may I suggest a couple of Mister Cooper's people draw the sharks to the bow using chum. The least amount of sharks at the stern may increase our chance of success." Menard suggested.

"That sounds like a plan. Make it happen!"

Cooper had sent an email to Michael Brady asking how he and his family liked Bermuda. He had also asked about the electrical beacon Bobbi had mentioned. She was obviously more up on events than he was. Cooper continued working through e-mails and then he got to one from Pamela Delaney, the chief financial officer of CISR. Her comments were short and sweet and the spreadsheet she sent along backed up her opinions. She was right and he knew it, but now was not the time to be worrying about funding for the Institute. Right now he had to worry about getting fifty-eight people home alive.

His mailbox pinged. An email from Snailsking462@gmail.com had just dropped into his inbox.

Michael Brady had written back. What the hell time was it in the Bermuda; 4:00 am? Michael had answered all of the family questions, briefly outlined the beacon and had attached a .jpeg of a schematic drawing he had done many years ago after the shark incident.

The tone of his e-mail was dry, not the friendly feeling he got from Bobbi's, but who was to blame him? The Coopers and the Brady's had been very friendly, but after Ritchie's death, the friendship faded.

It was a matter of woulda, coulda, shoulda, but that was all in the past. Michael thanked him for the generous donations over the years, but came straight out and said do not write him again. He had a new life in Bermuda and he never thought about Pearl Island or sharks.

Cooper wasn't surprised by Michael's tone or e-mail; he never got to know him or his younger brother Dean very well, but at least he cared enough to help fund Michael's research.

Cooper saved the schematic .jpeg to his hard drive, exited his mail program and opened it. The design was simple. It was rough but Michael had added notes along the margins of the drawing detailing changes that should be made to make it more effective. He had also sketched a small diagram of what a hand-held remote would look like. Not bad for a marine biologist who counts snails.

Cooper printed out the schematic and put the digital file on the company's mainframe in his personal folder. He would download it in the engineering lab and have Markowski, Amenta and one of the engineers take a look at it. They could cobble it together with what they had onboard in the engineering department's storage.

He had just closed his laptop when he started feeling the ship being hit, he didn't know by what, but he had a hunch. As the ship was still being hit he left his stateroom and headed down the hall towards the forward stairwell. The ship lurched hard a few times sending him to the carpeted floor.

"What the hell was that?"

The *Polaris II* was a large vessel, seventy-three meters in length with a gross tonnage of 3660. It took a lot to jar the ship, so whatever caused it to lurch like this was very big and dangerous.

Cooper got to his feet and felt a sharp pain in his right ankle, he must have rolled it when he fell to the deck.

He managed to get to the stairwell by leaning on the wall of the corridor and gingerly made his way up to the bridge deck. The ankle was feeling a little bit better, but it meant he would have go to Doctor Shane and have it looked at. He'd be lucky if he didn't leave the sickbay with more injuries. But first he needed to get to the bridge and find out what was wrong with the ship.

Cooper entered the rear of the bridge. Captain Dobbs saw him. "Do you see what your sharks are doing to my boat?"

"Sharks are doing this?" Cooper asked.

"They're all over the stern ramming the ship. A bunch of them jumped into the screws and damaged the propellers and drive shafts."

"Shit."

"Yes, *shit,* Mister Cooper."

Terrific, we were back to 'Mister' Cooper.

"What's your plan, Captain?"

"My plan is sending all my armed men to go on a shark hunt at the stern. Menard and Miss Jenkins are going down to engineering to get some underwater cameras to check out the damage. Once we see what it's like, we're going to have to decide to sit and wait for the Coast Guard, or try and fix at least one of the screws."

"I wouldn't recommend that, Cap, you'd just end up with more dead crewmen."

Dobbs' brows met in the middle and he gave Cooper a nasty stink-eye.

"Then what do you suggest we do, Mister Cooper?

Shit, the 'Mister' thing again.

"I've got a Plan A, a Plan B, and a hunch. I need to speak with Menard and then get down to engineering to see Amenta and Markowski about a bug zapper."

Cooper left the bridge in a hurry, favoring his ankle, leaving Captain Dobbs with a question on his face.

The days went by slowly as the shark herd followed the larger object. The snaggletooth had all of them swimming as close to the bottom as possible, to keep out of sight. When he saw that one animal looking at him, he felt there was intelligence there. He wanted to stay out of its way, but he felt the herd was dissatisfied and they were getting anxious. They needed to take this large prey so he could maintain control. He veered off and swam up, coming directly below the object, getting a read on it. He shook his head back and forth and then upwards. The herd broke into two packs, each one taking a side of the large prey. The attack was about to happen.

Chapter 38

XO Menard was ready at the stern rail with the modified underwater camera attached to the fishing gaff. He was joined by Lyla Jenkins and two of his crew members, Tim Bryant and Calvin Kerr, both crack shots. Menard had five of Cooper's shark researchers up near the bow with buckets of chum, ready to saturate the water with fish blood, chunks of fish and guts.

Jenkins had rigged a USB 3.0 cable to the camera with a nylon-braided cord for easy handling and connected it to her laptop for viewing and recording.

Menard was ready to submerge the camera and get whatever view they could of the damaged propellers, and his men were ready to shoot any sharks that came nearby. He radioed the science crew in the bow to start dumping the chum into the water. He would wait fifteen minutes before he attempted his task.

Menard's radio crackled after twelve minutes. The sharks were devouring the chum and the forward team counted at least sixty sharks in the water. Menard's two shooters reported no sharks in the water at the stern, so it was now or never.

Jenkins was ready, the camera was recording and Menard had the gaff almost into the water when a few sharks rushed up snapping at the camera. Shots range out from the armed crewmen and at least one shark was struck as blood spurted in the water. Menard thrust the gaff into the water and moved it around blindly, hopefully getting footage of the propellers and drive shafts. More shots rang out, but he was too busy focusing on getting the needed footage.

"How are we looking, Jenkins?" asked Menard.

"We're good, I think we have enough video for you to make

out the damage."

Jenkins saw the shark come at the camera but before she could say anything–

"Great, let me hoist this thing - *DAMN!*" shouted Menard.

The shark had taken the camera into its mouth pulling Menard overboard. Luckily, he let go of the gaff and grabbed the rail with one hand. His grip was a true death grip. If he let go, he would drop into the savage water below and end up like Higgins and Johnson.

Both sharpshooters were caught unaware and froze when they saw Menard go over. Jenkins had held onto the laptop, the video cable going taut and then snapping out of the computer. She saw Menard go over. She dropped the laptop and ran to the rail. When she looked over, she expected to see him in the water, but was surprised when she found him hanging by one hand on the middle rail, while trying his best to grab onto another rail with his other hand

"Let me help you up," she said.

Jenkins reached down with both hands and grabbed Menard's wrist, and helped him get a purchase on the rail. He slid over the rail onto the deck.

Both of them sat and leaned against the railing, exhausted and surprised that either of them was still alive.

"Remind me," Menard said. "When I have a stupid idea like this, to shut my mouth."

"Yes, sir," Lyla said with a smile.

Chapter 39

Captain Dobbs was sitting in his chair facing the rear hatchway when XO Menard and Jenkins came back onto the bridge.

"Did you enjoy your little romp back at the stern?"

"No comment, sir," Menard said, looking a bit sheepish.

Jenkins was playing it smart. She said nothing and kept her head down.

"Please tell me you got the footage we needed."

"We did sir, but you're not going to like it. Jenkins, show the Captain what we recorded."

Jenkins made her way over to her viewing station and queued up the footage she had uploaded to the ship's server. Menard and Dobbs joined her, looking over her shoulder.

Lyla pointed at her screen, "The footage is a bit shaky and the sharks didn't help but you can see here that-"

"That we're screwed," Captain Dobbs said.

The footage showed that one propeller was completely gone and the other only had one out of three blades intact. It also showed that the port drive shaft had a bend in it making it nearly impossible for full rotation without damaging the hull of the ship.

"That's terrific, Mister St. Onge?"

"Yes, Captain?"

"Get on the horn and contact the Australian Coast Guard. Find out where their closest ship is and how long it will take them to get to us under full steam. Emphasize dire straits and emergency status."

"Yes, sir."

"Captain, I recommend we get everyone inside, keep all the watches in place but all non-essential personnel and scientists stay in while we await rescue."

"I agree, Mister Menard, make it happen. Cooper wanted to speak with you earlier, so let's go fill him in on the state of his ship."

"*His* ship, sir?"

Dobbs shrugged his shoulders as he walked past his XO. "Yup. When it's in tip-top shape, it's my boat. When it's broken, it's his."

C·O·O·P·E·R
INDUSTRIES

Chapter 40

Pamela Delaney, CFO for the Cooper Institute for Shark Research, had called an emergency meeting of the Board of Directors of Cooper Industries. CISR was an entity unto itself; however CI governed it. She had received no response from the e-mail she sent to Matt Cooper days before.

That annoyed her.

What infuriated her though, were the reports she was getting from the research ship. They stated there had been two deaths onboard, the ship was damaged, the crew's lives were in jeopardy, and Mister Cooper was not doing anything about it being fixated on some strangely behaving sharks and one radioactive shark.

Radioactive?

She thought this must have been a typo but as she read more of the reports she found the statement to be true.

She felt it was in the Institute's best interest to call the meeting to discuss Cooper's behavior.

She was able to get almost all of the board members on such short notice, but she was missing Kate Loiselle and Kelly Scoles. One was on vacation in Alaska and the other was out on maternity leave. Both were able to call in on the conference line to learn what the meeting was about. The other eight members had made it to Florida and were ready to meet.

"Ladies and gentlemen, I'd like to call this meeting to order at 2:45, what say you?" The room filled with Ayes and Pamela began to outline the report she had sent to Matt Cooper, as well as the incoming reports from Australia.

"As you can see, financially we have some work to do, but when it comes to the situation in Australia, I feel there is only one solution that will bring our people safely home," she said.

"I feel it's time that Matthew Cooper steps down as CEO." This sent a buzz of whispers throughout the room. Edward Korovae raised his hand and Pamela recognized him.

"Miss Delaney, I've known Matt Cooper for thirty-five years and I respect his experience in the field of sharks and marine biology, along with his many accomplishments. If it were not for him, no one here at this table would have reaped the rewards they have over the past years, your self included. Did he not hire you away from a boring accounting position at a Big Pharma company?"

"He did–"

"And if it wasn't for the Cooper name and fortune, our stocks would not be where they are. Wasn't it Matt Cooper who took the company public?" continued Edward.

"It was–"

"Yet here you stand wanting to oust the man who started all of this? We know that sharking and the research our people do can be dangerous, but that does not give you the right to pull the plug when the seas get rocky!"

By this time Edward had risen to his six foot four inch height and was banging his fist on the boardroom's African mahogany conference table. He was in his seventies with a bald head ringed with short white hair. His closely clipped white goatee gave him an academic look, as did his hawk-like features. He was clearly angry about Pamela's decision and his time with the company afforded him this kind of display.

"Edward, please relax and sit down and let's discuss this... please?" asked Pamela.

Korovae took his seat and stared daggers at Pamela, but she was a professional at this and continued on.

"As you can all see, Edward is against my suggestion, but let me say this: this is just one incident, but the ramifications will snowball. We will have wrongful death lawsuits for the dead crewmen as well as civil suits, I'm sure, from other crew members who feel their lives were in danger."

Charles Sewell raised his hand to be recognized but didn't wait for Pamela's permission to speak.

"Pamela, as you know I work with the scientists and technicians throughout our two facilities and three vessels. I know them all and they have all signed Non Disclosure Agreements so I would like to know where you got your information from?"

Pamela looked at the Englishman who was challenging her. His dark hair and good looks swayed most people, but not her.

"Charles, I believe all the reports have been uploaded to our server system here in Florida."

"Pamela, I know for a fact that is not true. I was down in Information Technology earlier today going through the maintenance with the technicians and we have had no large uploads to our site. The Pearl Island facility has some file exchange with the *Polaris II*, but not us. Who has been leaking the information to you? Who is your spy, Miss Delaney?"

Pamela felt like she was losing control of the meeting that *she* had called. Between Korovae and Sewell, they had raised suspicions that there were other reasons for having Matt Cooper removed. She needed to fix this right now.

"Mister Sewell and Mister Korovae, you are both highly respected members of this board, and also in your own fields. I do not think you have the experience in managing such a widespread and profitable company as CISR," Pamela said.

She looked directly at Charles Sewell. "My information comes from a trusted employee onboard the *Polaris II* and I believe everything that I have read."

Neither man liked that, but stayed quiet while Pamela continued.

"If this Institute and all of its holdings plan to exist in ten years, then we need to make some changes, and in this case, the changes need to start at the top, no matter the history that the Chief Executive Officer holds.

Pamela stood triumphantly in front of the Board, "I propose

that Matthew Cooper be voted out as CEO." Pamela waited a beat to see how the room reacted, and then continued.

"He may stay on as a Board member with limited responsibilities, and we cash out his stocks in fifteen percent increments over the next twenty years."

"Mister Cooper will not be alive in twenty years," stated Korovae.

"That is not up to me, Edward. But I also think Mister Cooper will not be the only person on this board who will not be here in twenty years."

Edward's face was beet red with anger, but he refused to debate with her.

Pamela now addressed the entire board. "All I want is for this Institute to thrive. You've heard my statements, and those of others." She looked around the table. "You can all read the reports to verify my statements, or we can vote now on this matter. We all know that we need a two-thirds vote, aye or nay. So do we vote now, or do we wait and hope nothing else deadly happens in Australia?"

The board decided to vote. Matthew Cooper was out as CEO and an interim leader would be sought out. Korovae and Sewell were not happy about it and voiced it.

Pamela Delaney ended the meeting and thanked the Board members and retired to her office. She had a lot of work to do.

Chapter 41

Cooper was down in the Engineering Lab with Paper, Amenta and engineering specialist, Daniel 'Wez' Wesolowski. They were going over Michael Brady's diagrams

"I have to say Matt, your Doctor Brady came up with a great idea. It just needed some tweaking," explained Wez.

"How so?"

"His original beacon was cobbled together and he was goddamn lucky it worked. I'm surprised he wasn't shark food –"

Wez realized with whom he was sitting and what his boss, and mentor, Jon Johnson, meant to the others.

"Shit, I'm sorry guys…"

John Amenta said, "Don't worry about it, Wez. If JJ was here he would have said the same thing and without the apology."

"Keep going, Wez," said Cooper.

"So I looked at the notes Brady had left in the margins of his schematic. He was on the right track to making the beacon even better. I took his notes and with some of my Boston know-how improved on the improvements. We've got a wicked evil pulse beacon that will piss off any aquatic animal."

Paper said, "I'm really impressed with what Wez came up with. It's smaller than Brady's beacon. We were able to use some parts from the lab, and also used the 3D printer to create some of our own from scratch. All we have to do now is test it."

"And I suppose you want to do that here and now," said Cooper.

"I don't want to take it up on deck and have it fail. I'd be taking shit for months if it craps out," Wez said.

"Okay Wez, it's your toy, show us what you've got. Just don't set anything on fire."

Wez smiled and nodded at everyone in the lab. He was average height with glasses. He had short brown hair under his ever-present Boston Red Sox baseball cap. No one could remember ever seeing him without it.

He had brought down a small aquarium from the marine lab containing a few Crown Squirrelfish, a small reef dependent fish with lateral white lines along its coral body.

He placed the aquarium twelve feet away from the workbench where they were seated and then angled the pulse beacon in its direction.

The beacon looked like an old Chevy starter motor. It was cylindrical with one flat end. The other end had a molded end-cap with a few waterproofed wires coming out if it. These were attached to three terminals with stainless steel bolts.

One side of the cylinder had a flat flange with two threaded holes molded into it. This was one of the parts that had been 3D-printed. It looked like it could be mounted to a boat hull or even attached to a shark's stout dorsal fin.

Wez picked up the remote that Michael Brady had created. It had two toggle switches, two small idiot lights, a knurled knob that had all been 3D printed.

"Okay fellas, here we go."

Wez pointed the remote at the beacon, flipped one toggle switch. Its light lit up. The beacon had an internal battery and they could hear the brushes spinning inside, building up a charge. Wez had marked the knob from one to eleven and had turned it up to one.

He looked at Cooper and raised his eyebrows with a questioning expression. Cooper nodded his head. Wez flipped the second triggering toggle.

A piercing tone screamed through the lab making all the men wince in discomfort. What it did to the fish was something else. They were spastically convulsing in the water thrashing their heads from side to side. One even tried to leap out of the tank trying to escape the beacon's signal.

"Shut it down, Wez!" yelled Cooper.

Wez flipped off both toggles. The sound ended as the beacons internal brushes spun down. Once the pulse beacon stopped sending out its signal, the fish quieted down and resumed gently swimming in the tank.

"Well shit, that seems to work," said Amenta.

"And that was only set on *one*," Wez added. "Turn it up to eleven and you're going to be emitting a stronger and wider reaching pulse. It should drive every fish in the area crazy. Hopefully, it's enough to take care of every shark, including King Shark."

"I was hoping it would look like a ray gun or something," Paper admitted.

"Yeah, or some kind of cool Sith weapon," added Amenta, mimicking a light saber two-handed swing.

Wez looked at his two cohorts and shook his head in disgust. "You two are the worst," said Wez. He then turned to Cooper, "What do you think Matt?"

"Boys, I've spent the last forty years studying and protecting sharks and I hate to say this... let's go kill them. All of them."

Captain Dobbs and XO Menard found Cooper in the Engineering Lab and got him caught up with what happened with the underwater cameras and the state of the ship's propulsion. After that, Cooper was able to explain his ideas to the two senior officers.

"Gentlemen, we currently have a working model of the pulse beacon, which we've tested, and it works. But I want to keep it in check while we try something else."

"And what would that be?" asked Dobbs.

"I've spoken to Doctor Bissette and she has estimated a dosage of strychnine nitrate that if injected into King Shark, can kill it in sixty seconds."

Menard asked, "And how do plan to do that?"

"On normal sharks, if you can get them in the mouth or gills they're as good as dead. But because our boy is so big and its unsafe being in the water, I propose we shoot it with a shark dart containing an auto-loader filled with strychnine nitrate."

"That sounds far-fetched, Coop," said Dobbs.

"But not impossible," added Menard.

Dobbs turned to Menard, "How's that, XO?"

"I can rig one of our older rifles to take the dart and then hope we get a good shot."

"Do we have any crewman onboard who can make that shot?"

"You're looking at him, Cap."

Chapter 42

Doctor Shane had been busy the past few hours taking care of all the bumps and scrapes that the crew suffered during the shark attack on the ship. Most were superficial, but one of the mechanics in the engine room, Lou Guardino, had been too close to one of the bulkheads when the sharks hit. He had been thrown across the room into some storage crates, suffering severe whiplash and a bruised spine. She didn't think there were any fractures, but to be safe, she had him immobilized on a backboard until they could get him back to Brisbane and to an MRI machine to take a proper look.

For their own safety, she had sent all of her staff to their state-rooms. She would stay in the unit and keep an eye on everyone until they were asleep. Then she would have one of the nurses spell her so she could get some rest, but before that she wanted to check in on Himari. Shane walked to the far bed in the unit and drew back the privacy curtain. Himari was sitting up looking around her with a tired, but curious expression on her face.

"How are you doing, Himari?" asked Doctor Shane.

"Helen...where am...I? What is going...on?"

Himari was trying to get out of bed, so Shane tried to hold her back.

"How about you lay back down and get some rest. You've been through a lot and you have to give yourself time to heal."

"I feel better Doctor, really I do, just a little tired."

"That's good sweetheart, but I want you to rest. There's a lot going on and I don't want you getting stressed."

"It's the sharks isn't it?"

"How did you know?"

"I'm not sure, but I think I heard it somewhere. My head is still a little jumbled, but I remember hearing sharks and the ship is damaged and people are scared. Is that right Helen?"

"Yes, but I don't want you thinking about it. Just rest, okay?"

"Okay, Helen, I'll try and get some sleep."

Shane made sure Himari was settled back in her bed and then left to check on her other patients. Sleep never came to Himari because her mind started to put all the jumbled puzzle pieces together. She was starting to remember what happened. She remembered the sharks, and she remembered, Charlie.

Chapter 43

Cooper had joined Menard and crewman Bryant on the stern's lower deck. This was the lowest vantage spot for taking the shot that Cooper wanted. Menard had been able to modify three of the lab's shark darts with the auto-loader system suggested by Cooper. Matt had filled the internal chamber of the loader with the proper dosage of strychnine nitrate, and now it was just a matter of testing it out.

Bryant held two of the darts while Menard slipped the third dart's base over the rifle's barrel. The rifle he decided upon was the Ruger American .308 Winchester Bolt-Action Rifle. It had just the right pull-weight and wasn't a very heavy rifle, so reloading the darts would be quick.

"So where's your King Shark, Cooper?" Menard asked.

"Give it time, we just spread out a thick layer of chum. Now we wait for the sharks to get a good sniff of it."

"Dobbs is usually a patient man, but this whole shit show is stressing him out," said Menard.

"You know he's probably watching us," added Bryant.

All three men looked up at the CCTV camera mounted to the upper deck of the stern.

"Big brother is watching," said Bryant.

"More like big daddy and keep your comments to yourself, crewman," said Menard.

"Yes, XO."

It didn't take long for the chum to do its job. Sharks started coming around looking for a mid-day snack.

"Be ready with those darts, Bryant. I don't want to rely on just one lucky shot."

"Ready."

"There's our boy now," said Cooper, pointing behind them.

The huge dorsal fin of the shark cut through the water like a hot knife through butter, coming in from the right, heading for the stern. Menard was ready to fire, adjusting his grip on the trigger guard, waiting for his shot.

The large shark was starting to crest, showing more of his side when Menard pulled the trigger. The dart flew towards its target, looking to end the life of the shark, when a tiger shark suddenly breached in front of the dart and took it behind the gills. The tiger landed back in the water. It started to buck and convulse as it dropped below the waters surface.

"What the fuck was that!?" asked Menard as he looked over at Cooper. "Did that shark just take one for the team?"

"I have no idea. I've never seen that before."

"Bryant, give me another dart."

Menard fitted the dart onto the rifles' barrel, reloaded a shell, and threw the bolt. He was ready for another shot.

King Shark turned toward the stern, giving Menard a smaller target, but he took the shot anyway. The dart flew true, heading towards the shark's head when a great white surfaced in front of the larger shark and took the dart down its throat. Blood and tissue sprayed out the back of its head. With its spinal cord shredded, the great white quickly sank below the surface.

"Fuck me!" yelled Bryant.

Cooper was speechless almost unable to comprehend what he had just seen again, as he leaned on the rail.

"Cooper?" asked Menard.

"I don't know," he answered, staring out at the water.

"We've got one more dart, Mister Menard," said Bryant.

"Give it here. This fucker is *dead*."

He quickly reloaded the dart and threw the bolt. King Shark was moving away from them, picking up speed. It would dive below the surface at any time.

Menard quickly swung to his right, forcing Bryant to duck

below the barrel's path – when he set himself and pulled the trigger. The dart flew true – just as the shark started to dive. The tip of the shark's tail fin exploded as the dart passed through it. King Shark sank below the surface of the water with a flick of its bloody tail.

"Did you get it? Is it dead?" asked Bryant.

"Coop?" asked Menard as he looked over to the shark expert.

Cooper looked out to where the shark had disappeared, shook his head and said, "No."

"What do you mean, *NO?* We blew its tail off!" said Bryant.

"The dart has to go into tissue so the auto-loader can inject the poison. It was a nice shot, but just a flesh wound.

"Thanks, but explain that to the old man," said Menard.

They all looked behind them at the mounted camera.

After the men packed up and walked inside the diver's ready room, a service phone on the wall rang. Menard picked it up knowing who was on the other end.

"Yes, Captain."

"Nice shooting there, best I've ever seen."

Shit.

"Would you and Mister Cooper join me in the galley with his Plan B team so we can discuss our shark problem?"

"Yes, sir," replied Menard as he turned towards Cooper and Bryant.

"Is he pissed?" asked Cooper.

"He called you 'Mister' again. Walk with me."

"Shit."

Chapter 44

Cooper, Menard, and the pulse beacon team all met Dobbs in the galley to go over their plan for using the beacon. Joey T. had served them up some grilled cheese sandwiches and a hearty Thai basil tomato soup he had been cooking for six hours. This crew needed comfort food and the chef had delivered.

"Gentlemen," started Captain Dobbs, "Plan A did not work so you are on to Plan B. Mister Cooper, would you care to start us off?"

"Yes, sir. What we need, is to get the pulse beacon in the water and then set it off. It should drive the sharks crazy and hopefully force them away."

"And where do you want to do this? I'm assuming you want to use the shark cradle?"

"I think it's the best place to submerge the beacon. We can keep the cradle high enough out of the water to keep our people safe and still get the beacon into the water."

"You know I'm not crazy about anyone being that close to the water, but if you think that's our best option, then let's make it happen."

Menard turned to Cooper and asked, "How many of my guys will you need to pull off this stunt?"

"Hey, man, if this 'stunt' works, we'll be saving everyone's asses," said Wez.

"I'm not trying to shit on your parade, Wez, but so far everything we've tried has failed, so call me a pessimist."

Cooper stepped in to avoid any distractions. "I think we're going to need a couple of deck hands to keep watch. Your guys with rifles will help just in case we get into trouble," stated Cooper.

"And I'll be there, too, just in case you try and get yourself eaten again," answered Menard.

"I'm glad you said that," replied Cooper, "Because I'm the one that's going to hang the beacon over the side of the ship."

"Matthew, why you?" asked Dobbs.

"Because, Cap, this is my company's excursion and I own this boat and employ everyone at this table. I will be damned if another one of my people is put in harm's way."

Dobbs said, "Don't take this personally, Matt, but you're no spring chicken. You may be in good shape, but we're talking dangerous animals here."

"Cap, I've been in dangerous situations before and I'm still alive to talk about them. This is the deal, I'm doing this."

After everything had been said, they finished their meals and started to walk out of the galley when Amenta came up behind Markowski.

"Big fucking balls," John said quietly.

"No shit, brother. Cooper will either be a hero or a meal," Paper said.

Chapter 45

Himari awakened from her nap and felt clearer than she had in days. She remembered everything that happened to the ship, the crew, and to her Charlie. She had done enough sleeping and needed out of this hospital bed. She was wearing a hospital gown and treaded socks, so if she was leaving she needed some clothes. She found a set of hospital scrubs in a closet next to her bed. She put them on and peaked around her privacy curtain. Doctor Shane had left to get some sleep and there were two nurses on duty looking after the patients. Neither was looking her way so she quietly crept out of the sickbay.

She followed the corridor until she came to the rear stairway and then made her way up to the next deck. She was now at the door to the diver's ready room. The doors were open and she saw some of the crew on the stern deck. They were talking very animatedly. She quietly stepped into the ready room to listen to the conversation.

Captain Dobbs had assembled a small crew on the stern deck just in front of the shark cradle. With him were Steve Menard, Matt Cooper, Wez Wesolowski, Paper Markowski, John Amenta, Abigail Bissette, and crewmen Kerr and Bryant. Both of them had won awards in the service for marksmanship. Dobbs wanted to be ready if things went bad. He had to keep his crew safe.

Kerr and Bryant had taken position on opposite corners of the rail above the shark cradle while Menard was working the hydraulics to lower the cradle to a level just above the water. Once set, he locked the controls and joined the others as they neared the cradle. Cooper had the pulse beacon in his arms and Wez had the remote. Markowski brought over a long handled gaff and he and

Cooper used stainless steel zip-ties to secure it to the gaff's hooked end. Matt gave the rigged beacon a couple of hard shakes and deemed it ready to go. He was wearing a wet suit to keep dry and water shoes to maintain a grip on the slick cradle decking.

"I'm going to the end of the cradle and dip the beacon in. Wez, I want you to hit the switch and dial it up to seven. We need to see how the sharks react. If we have to, juice it all the way up."

"I got it, boss."

"The rest of you watch my ass, I have no desire to be fish food."

"Matthew," said Captain Dobbs. Matt turned to his old friend as he came up to him and gripped his shoulders. "Be careful out there."

Cooper looked at his friend and smiled, "Thanks Bob."

"Cooper," Menard said with a shit-eating grin, "My knees are still hurting me so don't do anything stupid."

"Right."

Matt looked at the assembled men and woman, nodded at all of them, then stepped down to the shark cradle and hesitantly started across it. He could see shark fins breaking the surface of the water and he was damn scared. What the Hell was he doing out here? He thought back a few mornings and realized he asked himself the same thing then. He glanced back at the crew and saw that they had all stepped closer to the cradle. He knew they had his back, but they were only human. These sharks were something else entirely.

He had made it to the rail when he heard crunching. He looked to his right and saw the massive head of a great white gnawing at the wooden edge of the cradle decking. A smaller Mako started to chew on the cradle boards next to it . The only thing keeping them at bay was the height of the platform. He looked to his left and saw no sharks there, so he continued towards the edge of the cradle and the short wall at the end of it. It was this same wall that he went over when Menard tried to save him from the great white only a few days ago.

Cooper would rather not relive the past. He leaned against the cradle wall and swung the gaff and beacon over the edge, into the water.

Cooper yelled over his shoulder, "Wez, now!"

Wesolowski flipped the first toggle to get the beacon motor primed, dialed the intensity to seven, and flipped the trigger switch.

Cooper felt, more than heard, the pulse rush up the aluminum pole, but he could see that the sharks had heard it. The two gnawing on the cradle started to convulse. When he looked out at the water, it was churning with shark bodies. All of them felt the pulse, and all of them were in pain.

Suddenly the water exploded as King Shark breached the surface. Everyone gasped when they saw a creature that big break the surface of the water and then come crashing back down. Cooper was drenched with the backwash of the shark's reentry and almost lost his grip on the gaff.

"How do you like the pain you shit-heads!" he yelled.

The crew behind him were hooping and hollering when Cooper felt thumps against the cradle. The hits started to increase and he felt the cradle start to sway. Cooper was scared, and his face paled. Sharks were swimming up and ramming the cradle deck. More sharks appeared in the water and started towards the ship, and towards him. The two sharks to his right were inching their way up onto the cradle when a big hammerhead breached to his left and landed on the deck, eyeing him like an aged piece of meat.

Matt turned to the others, "Shit! Wez, turn off the beacon!"

Cooper pulled the beacon out of the water and cautiously stumbled across the deck towards safety. Wez had shut the beacon off and the internal brushes wound down.

Menard and Paper reached forward and pulled Cooper up from the cradle to safety.

Captain Dobbs yelled out to the sharpshooters. "Bryant! Kerr! Kill those fucking sharks! Get them off my deck!"

The shooters started to fire at the three sharks on the cradle. Bryant was shooting a Smith & Wesson, M&P15 while Kerr was using a Ruger, SSR-556. Both weapons were semi-automatics. The men were pacing their shots, especially with so many of the crew directly below.

Once the deck was cleared of the three sharks, the men began to shoot into the water when they saw heads or fins break the surface. With the beacon turned off the sharks seemed to recover, disappearing below the waves, but not before King Shark drew alongside the ship and slapped the hull with its damaged tail fin, marking it with his blood. A few of the crew were also hit by the shark's blood. He sank below the surface before either marksmen could take a shot.

The giant shark's pain was getting worse. He knew he was dying, but he needed to finish what he started. Blood and small prey had been dumped into the water along the floating object. This started a feeding frenzy and there was nothing he could do to control it. He saw his brothers feeding, but he also saw some of them dying and sinking downward. Those sharks that were not feeding in the middle of the packs were scavenging the dead or dying. This disgusted him. He had not eaten another shark since his birth, no matter how hungry he got. His body was consuming itself and he needed to feed it from a different source. He picked up speed and decided to attack the large object himself. The giant surfaced behind his prey and he saw the object. It was huge, larger than he could imagine. He thought he might not be able to take it on himself, but was determined to try. He saw smaller prey moving along the rear of it. They looked like the prey that he had seen earlier in the water.

Prey.
Prey filled with blood, flesh and oils. He wanted them...he needed them!

Chapter 46

Doctor Shane was back in the sickbay keeping her patients as calm and comfortable as possible. Everyone heard the thumping on the ship's hull. The scuttlebutt had already started, with rumors running rampant about sharks sinking the ship and eating everyone.

She had a call in to Captain Dobbs to find out what was going on, but she was told he was off the bridge. The same went for Menard and Cooper. If it weren't for her patients, Shane would have hunted down the senior staff to give them a good piece of her mind. She finally decided to check on Himari. Shane was hoping the poor girl was asleep and getting the rest her body, and mind, needed.

She peeked around the privacy curtain and saw an unmade bed and dressing gown, but no Himari. She looked all over her ward, but there was no sign of the marine biologist. This had her worried because she knew Himari was in no condition to be wandering around. She went back to her office and called up to the bridge to let them know Himari was wandering the ship and for the crew to keep an eye out for her. For now, that was all she could do.

Chapter 47

"What the hell was that, Coop?" yelled Captain Dobbs.

"I have no idea Cap," answered Cooper.

Both men were face-to-face on the rear deck, Dobbs was irate.

"It looked to me like your sharks got pretty pissed off with the beacon and wanted to eat it," said Menard.

"I can't see how that would happen," said Wez.

"Maybe it affected the fish in the lab differently 'cause they're not as developed as sharks," suggested Paper.

"Wez, you said you tried the beacon on smaller fish?" asked Abigail.

"Yeah, we had a couple squirrelfish in the marine lab, so I put them in a tank and tried the beacon out on them. They went crazy, convulsing, swimming like they were in pain."

Abigail thought about if for a minute, walked around the deck, and then looked at the group of men and made a decision.

"I think Paper is right. These sharks are on a different level than your normal sharks. Maybe King Shark has something to do with it. He was strangely affected by the beacon."

"And the sharks came for me, so wherever the beacon is, the sharks will follow...," added Cooper.

"That makes sense. They thought the beacon was the cause of their pain and then targeted it."

"That's all fine and dandy but how does that help us out?" asked Dobbs.

"I've got a crazy idea that none of you are going to like...," said Paper.

"Spit it out, man!" said Dobbs.

Paper looked at everyone, not sure about his idea, he decided to go for it.

"What if we get the beacon onto King Shark and let him draw the other sharks away from us?"

"Do you think that will work?" asked Amenta.

"Maybe," said Paper. " But first we gotta figure out how to get it on him."

Crewman Bryant yelled down from the upper rail. "If you're going to do something, do it quick because he's back and he's brought a lot of friends!"

They all looked up as Bryant pointed behind them. They saw the big dorsal fin that could only have belonged to King Shark. It was swimming behind them and slowly moving up alongside the cradle. The *Polaris II* was still moving forward even without its screw turning. The momentum of its course and the current slowly pushed it along. More shark fins appeared alongside the ship and a large group of them gathered around King Shark, almost like bodyguards around a celebrity.

"My god! Cooper, are they parallel swimming the ship?" asked Abigail.

"That's not possible – is it?" Matt asked, turning to Abigail.

"Hey shark nerds, can you speak English for the rest of us?" asked Wez.

Abigail looked over at Wez with a disappointed look. She needed to keep her focus on the sharks.

Abby raised her hands palm to palm and moved them forward and backwards. "Parallel swimming is when two sharks swim side-by-side, sizing each other up. Usually the smaller of the two will relent and swim away, but sometimes they don't and the bigger one has to show him who's the boss."

"And that's what they're doing out there –?" asked Wez.

"I think so."

"So who's the boss?" asked Wez.

"Tony Danza," answered Paper, with a big smile.

Wez looked up at the big man with a *are you serious?* expression.

"That was pretty quick, big guy," said Amenta, slapping Paper on the shoulder.

"Thanks."

"Enough you three. Cooper, what do you make of that?" asked Menard.

"If Abigail's right then we haven't any time to lose. The entire herd is going to treat us like a smaller shark and eventually attack us on a grand scale."

Bryant yelled out again. "The big one is moving behind us but the other sharks are staying alongside the ship."

"We don't have much time, Captain," Cooper said.

Bryant looked down to the group. "Now the big one is weaving back and forth!"

Captain Dobbs stepped forward to make sure everyone heard him.

"I want to be sure we're all on the same page here. Goal number one is to keep us all alive. Goal number two is to keep this ship from being damaged anymore than it is. If anyone has any useful ideas on how to get the beacon onto that big-ass shark, then speak up now."

"I know how, Captain –"

Himari came out of the diver's ready room wearing a wetsuit, water shoes and work gloves, jogging past everyone until she got to Cooper. She paused, grabbed the beacon mounted gaff, looked him straight in the eye and said, "I've got this."

She then sprinted along the deck with the gaff in hand. She dropped down to the shark's cradle deck and sprinted towards the short wall facing the ocean, and King Shark.

"Himari, no!" yelled Cooper.

"What's she doing?"

"She's nuts!"

Chapter 48

When Himari Kohi was a young girl living in Kagoshima, Japan, her parents enrolled her in a gymnastics class after school, and she took to it quickly. She was small, strong and was very good on the parallel bars and vaults. As she ran across the deck she knew what she had to do. She would make sure the beacon was on King Shark, even if she had to hold it onto the beast.

As she ran, King Shark swam to her left, coming very close to the shark cradle, in his effort to swim parallel with the ship. This was Himari's chance. She leapt onto the wall, planted one foot, and then sprung as far as she could.

She landed on King Shark's back directly behind his dorsal fin, and threw her leg over the shark's pine, riding him like a horse.

From its back, she could see how diseased the animal was. Its skin, covered in dermal denticles, was soft and spongy instead of being hard and sharp. Where she landed she could see the denticles sloughing off into the water. King Shark must have been in terrible pain – he didn't even register the one hundred and twenty pound woman landing on his back. She turned the gaff so the sharp hooked end pointed at the dorsal fin. With all of her strength, she rammed the point into the soft, diseased flesh. The sharp end came out the other side of the huge fin with a spray of blood and pus. The muscle was deteriorated, allowing the gaff to go in easily. With the hooked gaff in its fin, King Shark bucked and thrashed its rear body and tail, trying to shake off the new pain, but it didn't work. Himari pushed the gaff in even more and got another response from the shark.

"This is for my Charlie, you bastard!"

It had turned back around behind the ship and was circling. She now had the beacon attached to the shark, but had no way of escape, especially with so many sharks swimming around. King Shark was bleeding and the other sharks began to sense the blood in the water.

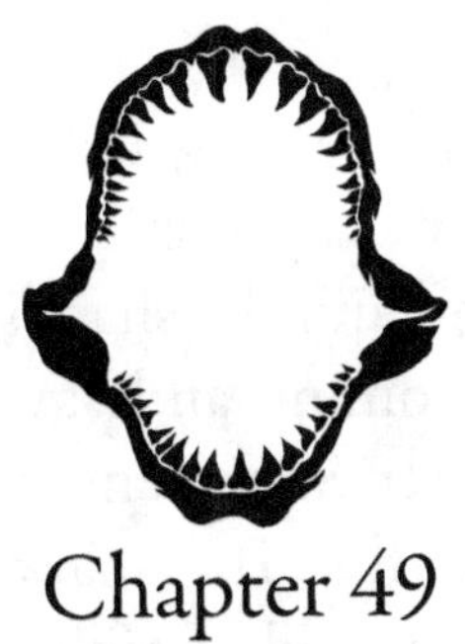

Chapter 49

PAIN!...PAIN!...PAIN! Something was stabbing him in his dorsal fin and an animal had landed on him. The thing in his fin sent a pulse of pain through his entire body. He was losing control. He could barely see where he was swimming. He bucked and twisted, but he could not shake the animal off of him.

Everyone was at the stern rail watching Himari's act of bravery.

"Jesus Christ, what is she doing?" yelled Dobbs.

"She's saving our asses!" yelled Cooper. "Wez, get the beacon up and running!"

Wez flipped on the first switch and had his fingers on the dial when he asked, "How high do you want it?"

"*Spinal Tap* it!"

With a surprised look, Wez answered, "Okay!"

"How the hell are we going to get her off the shark?" asked Paper.

XO Menard looked around for some way to reach Himari. He saw the cargo boom and got an idea. He ran up the stairs one level to the hydraulics station that controlled the crane. The steel cable ended in a cargo hook, which had an old truck tire above it for protection. It was the perfect platform for Himari to grab onto.

Menard yelled down. "Everyone step back! Wez, get ready to zap that fucker!"

Menard manned the hydraulics controls and swung the crane out over the water, extending the boom as far out as it would go. It sat forty-five feet out past the shark cradle. He dropped the hook almost down to the waters surface.

King Shark was still circling behind the ship and drawing closer to the stern. Himari was balancing as well as she could, holding onto the gaff with one hand and the shark's dorsal fin with the other. She saw the crane hook coming and saw her escape, but she still needed to get the shark closer. She wrenched back the gaff, skewering the hook further into the fin. The shark bucked savagely, almost throwing Himari off, but she held on tight.

Cooper saw the opening and looked over to Wez.

"Give it a quick zap!"

Wez flipped the trigger switch on for a few seconds, and then off.

King Shark threw his head back and sprayed water into the sky. Himari had felt the beacon trigger and she raised both hands away from it. She felt a tingling in her legs that startled her. She decided it was time to leave. The shark started to go under, and Himari knew that would be her end if he did.

"Again!"

The switch was flipped again and the shark would have screamed out in pain if it could. Fire ran up and down its body, starting at its Ampullae of Lorenzini and ending at its tail fin.

"Turn it off, Wez. I don't want to hurt Himari!" yelled Cooper.

Himari saw more skin and tissue sloughing off the great beast's body. She thought she saw blood spraying from the shark's mouth. What she was certain of, though, was that the shark was heading directly towards the *Polaris II* and the crane hook.

"Menard, get ready, here she comes!" yelled Cooper.

"Come on girl, you got this!" yelled Amenta.

"This better work!" shouted Paper.

King Shark headed directly for the shark cradle. Even though the pulse beacon had stopped transmitting, the searing pain had intensified, blinding its vision and smothering its other senses.

Himari saw the crane hook coming up fast as Menard started to raise it higher for her. She got onto her haunches and was ready to leap when she started to see other sharks swimming beside the big shark.

They were bumping and posturing the shark and acting aggressively towards it. It was only a matter of time before they either attacked or retreated.

The crane's tire was in reach. Himari leapt and grabbed onto the tire and swung upwards away from King Shark. She looked over at Menard and gave him a thumbs up. He began to raise the crane and bring in the boom.

King Shark kept coming on strong until he struck the shark cradle, breaking through the short wall, bending the cradle's metal frame, splintering it's wooden deck. As he hit the cradle the other sharks broke off and swam away to a safe distance.

Everyone on deck stumbled due to the collision; Amenta fell and wrenched his knee, Captain Dobbs stumbled backwards against a storage cabinet, striking his head. Crewman Bryant struck the rail hard on his hip, losing his balance and going over into the water. He didn't have time to scream as he hit, knocking him unconscious, and saving him the pain of tearing flesh and bone.

Himari held onto the crane's tire for dear life. When the collision caused the crane cable to sway in the air, her body whipped-around like a yo-yo in the wind.

"Menard, bring her in!" yelled Cooper.

"I'm trying! The boom is off balance!"

Cooper looked down at the shark. It was chewing the deck of the cradle. He could see that a lot of its teeth had snapped off. Blood was spewing from its mouth but that failed to stop the animal's instinct to bite. Cooper looked over to Captain Dobbs, who was on deck holding the back of his head in pain. He saw he was in no condition to make any decisions. Menard was focused on getting Himari back onboard, so it was now or never if they wanted to save the ship and its crew.

The giant swam away from the floating object. He had rammed it and hurt himself. His head felt like it was in pieces, cartilage plates rubbing against each other sending fiery pain throughout his head. Pain screamed all the way down his lateral line. He felt his insides flowing out of him. His skin burned all over, causing him to writhe in pain.

Cooper turned to Wez, "Hit the beacon!" but the engineer was no longer at the rail.

Wez was scurrying after the remote. It has been knocked out of his hands and was sliding towards the water. He dived at the last minute, losing his coveted Red Sox cap. He got his fingers on the remote, hugging it to his chest. He looked at Cooper with a sigh of relief and scrambled back to Cooper's side.

"Hit the beacon, Wez!"

"How long?"

Cooper looked him square in the eyes and said, *"Fry the fucker."*

Wez flipped the first switch, made sure the dial was on eleven then flipped the trigger. Everyone could hear the whine of the beacon and saw what it was doing to King Shark.

It was thrashing in spasms from the pain; blood now visibly spraying from its mouth, eyes and gills. The crewmembers could see the damage the creature had done to itself when it hit the cradle. It's jaws were clearly broken and the remainder of it's teeth on one side were all gone. In his thrashing its belly was exposed. The usually light grey skin was splotched with blood; it was oozing out of his skin. The radiation poisoning had fully taken hold, and its internal organs were liquefying.

Menard finally got the crane under control and was able to bring Himari down close enough to the stern deck that she dropped and rolled to safety. Paper and Abigail ran over to help her up while crewman Kerr sprinted into the ready room for a dry blanket to keep her warm.

Cooper came over to her with mixed emotions, angry with her for being so reckless with her life, and proud that she had the strength and courage to do what she did. He grabbed both of her shoulders and congratulated her.

"You did it, Himari!"

"Thank you, Mister Cooper. I had to do something," she replied.

"You did more than just something, Doctor," said Dobbs as he came over to them, still holding his head. "You saved us *and* this boat."

Amenta got to his feet with Paper's help, trying to keep his weight off his injured knee. Together they looked back out at King Shark. He was still thrashing and bucking in pain and headed away from the boat.

"Hey guys, it's swimming away," said Paper.

"Look! The other sharks are going after it!" cried Amenta.

The pulse beacon was not only affecting King Shark, but the other sharks as well. All were in severe pain and they wanted to make it stop. Targeting the larger shark as the source of their pain, they began to attack it, ripping and tearing large chunks of its flesh. Pools of blood, ichor and tissue were left in the sharks' wake; its internal organs now all but fluid. Only its will to escape the pain kept it moving.

Eventually the herd of sharks had taken so much of its tissue and muscle that the larger shark could no longer swim. It began to sink and drown. The last thing the crewmembers saw was its dorsal fin sinking below the waves with the beacon and gaff still piercing its skin. All the other sharks followed it.

XO Menard came over to Himari, and she gave him a big hug.

"Thank you for saving me," she whispered into his chest.

"My pleasure, anytime. Now let's get you looked at by Doctor Shane. I'm sure she's worried about you. While we're there, I'll have one of my guys sweep us for any radiation. I don't think we have anything to worry about, but your riding that shark and now hugging me, might give us cause to get checked out"

"Oh, Steve, I am so sorry. I didn't mean to expose you–"

"Don't worry about it, let's go inside." Menard put his arm around her shoulder, and they retreated into the diver's ready room, and headed down to sickbay.

Captain Dobbs turned to Cooper, "I guess you don't have any corpse to dissect, Matthew."

"No, Bob, I don't suppose I do. But to be honest with you, I'm okay with it."

Dobbs put his hand on Cooper's shoulder and the two old men smiled and looked out at the sea and saw the sun starting to set.

"How about I buy you a drink?" Dobbs asked.

"My friend, that's the best thing I've heard all damn day."

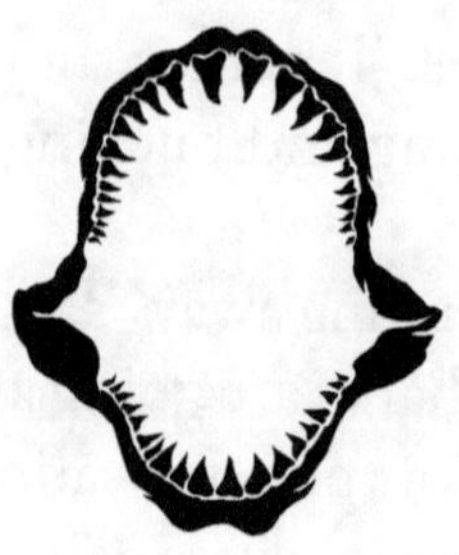

The animal on his back was gone, but he was still suffering. The pulsing in his fin was still there and he was getting weaker. He could barely make sense of anything. He was swimming away from the floating object, when he started to feel bites on his fins. His brothers had smelled his vulnerability and were attacking him. What was left of the herd was feasting on his diseased flesh. He shook his body trying to fend them off, but he was unable to.

It did not matter how big he was, the numbers were taking him down. His body fluids continued to flow and his muscles began to twitch and spasm. He dropped below the surface and planed downward. Large chunks of his flesh had been torn from his body, so he did not have enough muscle and connective tissue to keep moving. His body was numb, consciousness was fading and the constant pulsing through his body had finally started to wane. The only thing keeping him breathing was his downward motion, forcing water over his gills. Eventually even that wouldn't be needed much longer. Blind, bleeding, with all his senses failing, the giant snaggletooth slipped into unconsciousness, and died before he reached the bottom of the sea.

Chapter 50

To: bcooper@cisr.com
From: mcooper@cisr.com

Subject: Brisbane sharks

Hi Bobbi,

I'm still alive, the boat is still afloat, and King Shark is dead.

It's a long story that I'll tell you later on. The Australian Coast Guard is sending out a cutter to evacuate most of the staff and crew. The *Polaris II* will have to be towed in and dry docked for repairs. Captain Dobbs estimated 4-6 months of work and she'll be ready to go back into service.

Dobbs has told me confidentially, that this is his last trip. He's going to retire back to Massachusetts and relax with his family. I will miss the old fart; he was a good skipper and will always be a friend.

Steve Menard will be taking over as Captain and he'll need his own XO. Maybe your friend Kris would be up to the position? You could always sign on for six months and see what happens.

Regrettably, we did not recover King Shark's body for examination. As far as I know, it's sunk to the bottom of the Coral Sea, along with the pulse beacon.

I'll be back in Florida in a week or so, and then I'll head up to Pearl. Let's make plans to have dinner and I'll bring you all of the reports so you can look them over.

I have a funny feeling things will be changing at CISR. I'm tired and I think this is going to be my last trip too. It's time for just one Cooper to be chasing sharks across the oceans.

Love you lots,
Matt

Doctor Matthew Cooper
Cooper Institute for Shark Research
Miami, FL

Mark Masztal is an award-winning illustrator and designer. He is known in the comic book field as the artist and co-creator of the Shar-Pei series, recently collected as the *Chronicles of Shar-Pei*, and as the creator of the space opera, NOMAD.

He was lead book designer on John Rovnak's massive volume, *Panel To Panel: Exploring Words & Pictures Volume 1*.

He was also the designer and artist for G. Michael Dobbs' *15 Minutes With*, letterer on Stephen Murphy & Michael Zulli's, Eisner Award nominated *The Collected Puma Blues* and designer on Stephen Murphy's Eisner Award nominated *Umbra* collection.

Along with Mike Dobbs, Mark is the co-founder of Bing Comic Con, a 1-day pop culture event in Springfield, MA.

Mark was born and raised in Massachusetts, where he lives with his understanding wife Kathy and his dog, Cady. He spends his spare time volunteering for and representing Greyhound Options as their Vice President.

This is his first novella.

He can be found at www.masztal.com, and on Facebook and Instagram.

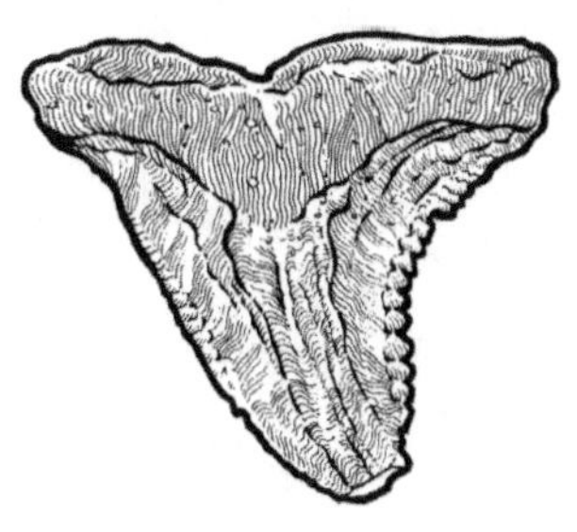

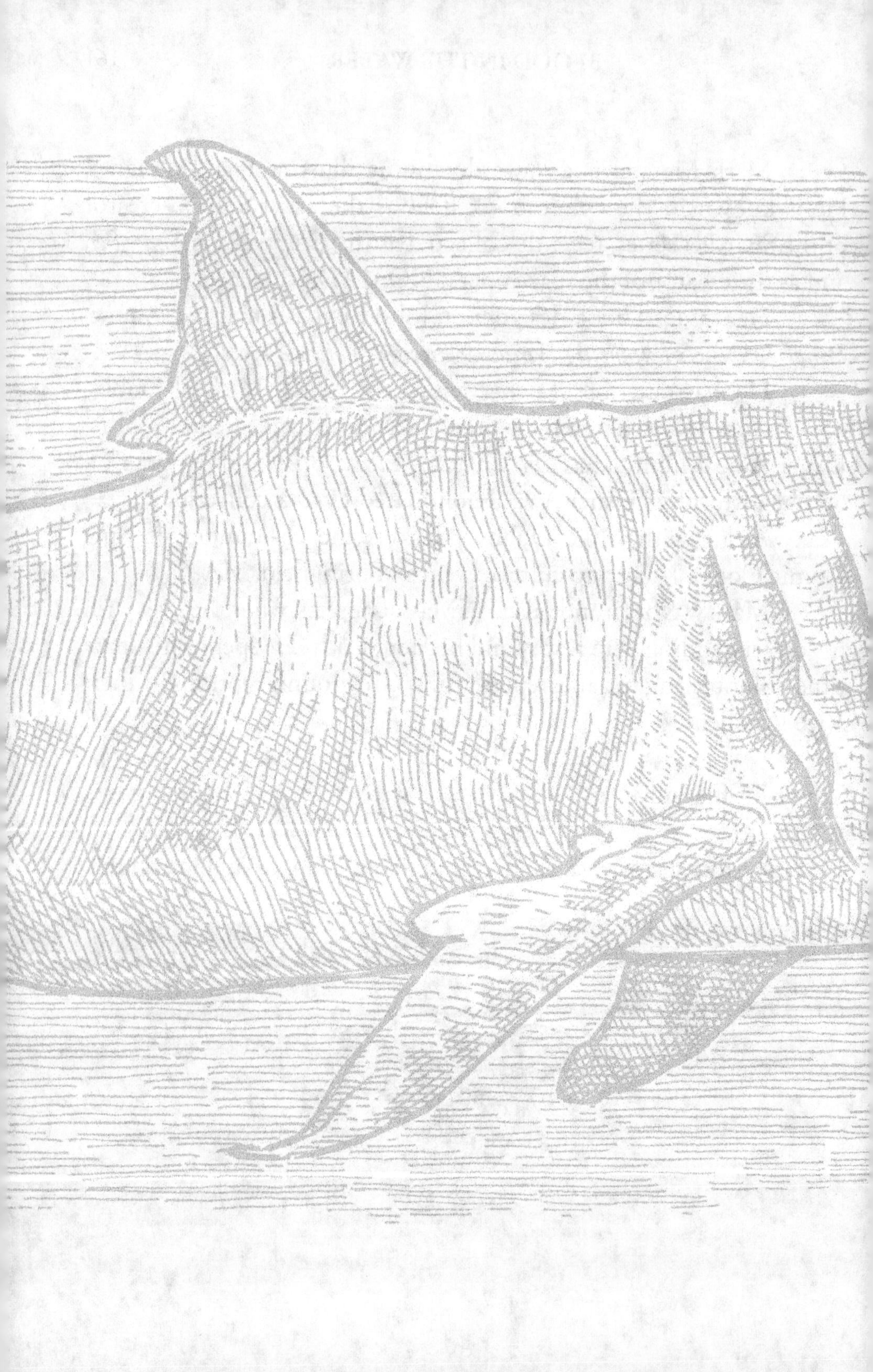

www.ingramcontent.com/pod-product-compliance
Lightning Source LLC
Chambersburg PA
CBHW071522100726
47908CB00004B/1259